U0010322

彼得潘
PETER PAN

詹姆斯·馬修·巴利◎著
辛一立◎譯
詹艷玲◎圖

晨星出版

愛藏本 090

彼得潘【中英雙語版】
Peter Pan

作　　者｜詹姆斯·馬修·巴利（James Matthew Barrie）
譯　　者｜辛一立
繪　　者｜詹艷玲

責任編輯｜陳品蓉
文字校對｜陳品蓉、許仁豪、呂曉婕
美術編輯｜林素華
封面設計｜鐘文君

創 辦 人｜陳銘民
發 行 所｜晨星出版有限公司
　　　　　行政院新聞局局版台業字第 2500 號
總 經 銷｜知己圖書股份有限公司
地　　址｜台北 台北市 106 辛亥路一段 30 號 9 樓
　　　　　TEL：02-23672044 ／ 23672047　FAX：02-23635741
　　　　　台中 台中市 407 工業區 30 路 1 號
　　　　　TEL：04-23595819　FAX：04-23595493
　　　　　E-mail: service@morningstar.com.tw
　　　　　http://www.morningstar.com.tw
法律顧問｜陳思成律師
出版日期｜西元 2018 年 03 月 15 日（二版）
郵政劃撥｜15060393
戶　　名｜知己圖書股份有限公司
讀者服務專線｜04-23595819#230

印　　刷｜上好印刷股份有限公司

定　　價｜新台幣 250 元
ISBN 978-986-443-414-5
Publishing by Morning Star Publishing Inc.
Printed in Taiwan

國家圖書館出版品預行編目資料

彼得潘（中英雙語）／詹姆斯·馬修·巴利（James Matthew
Barrie）著；辛一立譯；詹艷玲繪 —— 二版.
臺中市：晨星，2018
愛藏本；90
譯自：Peter Pan
ISBN 978-986-443-414-5（平裝）
CIP 873.59　107001790

彼得‧潘

PETER PAN

目次

第一章　彼得潘出現

所有的小孩都會長大，只有一個人例外。溫蒂是這樣知道的：兩歲時的某一天，她在花園裡玩耍，摘下一朵花兒跑向母親。達林太太抱住她說：「唉，真希望妳永遠只是個孩子！」關於成長這個話題，她們沒再多說什麼，但溫蒂從此知道，自己是一定要長大的。

他們住在門牌14號的屋子，在溫蒂出生之前，達林太太一直是家裡最重要的人。

她是位迷人的女子，有一顆浪漫的心及一張甜蜜卻又愛嘲弄人的嘴。

達林太太穿著白衣出嫁。最初，她詳細地記錄家庭收支，開開心心地把記帳當成一種遊戲；雖然遺漏一顆抱子甘藍並不有趣。但不久，她就連大棵的花椰菜都漏記了，取而代之出現在帳簿上的，是許多沒有面貌的小嬰兒畫像。

溫蒂是頭一胎，其次是約翰，最後是麥可。

達林太太對現狀心滿意足，但達林先生卻渴望能跟鄰居一樣——這代表他們也得

有一個保姆。孩子的牛奶開銷驚人，造成他們生活貧困，所以他們找來的保姆是隻乾淨的紐芬蘭犬，名叫娜娜。牠總是很重視孩子。在達林一家收留牠之前，娜娜是隻無家可歸的流浪狗。達林一家人是在肯辛頓花園遇見娜娜的。事實證明，牠的確是個好保姆。牠會細心周到地幫孩子洗澡；午夜時，只要孩子發出細微的哭聲，牠就會立刻起身查看。當然，牠的狗窩就在育兒室裡。牠有一種天份，能夠分辨哪一種咳嗽聲無須理會，哪一種又代表你的脖子上得加條圍巾。看牠護送孩子們上學就等於是在上禮儀課，孩子們守規矩時，牠會沉靜地走在一旁，一旦有孩子走偏了，牠就會趕他們回隊伍裡。

沒有一間育兒室比達林家的更井井有條了——達林先生也知道這一點，但有時他還是會多心，懷疑鄰居在背後說閒話。他總得顧慮自己在城裡的地位啊！

關於娜娜，達林先生煩惱的其實還有一點——有時，他會覺得娜娜不夠尊敬他。

「喬治，我知道娜娜很尊敬你。」達林太太向他保證，然後示意要孩子對父親特別敬重。於是，孩子們跳起可愛的舞蹈討父親歡心。有時，他們僅有的另一個僕人麗莎也會一起參與；儘管達林夫婦僱用麗莎時，她發誓自己已經超過十歲了，但穿著長裙戴著傭人帽的麗莎看來就像個小矮人。再也沒有哪個家庭比達林一家更單純更快樂的了

——直到彼得潘的到來。

達林太太第一次聽到彼得潘的名字，是在她替孩子們整頓心靈之時——這是每個好母親夜晚會做的工作，如果孩子的心靈是抽屜，那麼記憶就如同內衣與襪子，需要好好地折疊整齊放好。

孩子的心靈地圖如同你的體溫紀錄表，上面滿是鋸齒狀的線條，那些線條可能就是島嶼上的道路；「夢幻島」應該可算是個島嶼，周圍的海面上有著珊瑚岩和外型靈巧的小船，島上則佈滿各種色彩，有河流穿越其中的山谷和快要腐爛的茅屋，那裡住著野蠻人、孤單的說謊者、多半以裁縫維生的侏儒，還有六個兄弟的王子，以及一個有著鷹勾鼻、身材矮小的老太太。

每個孩子的夢幻島都不太一樣。約翰住在一艘翻覆在沙灘上的船裡，麥可住在印地安人的小屋，溫蒂則住在一間由葉子巧妙地搭蓋成的屋子裡。約翰獨來獨往，麥可的朋友會在晚上出現，溫蒂則養了一隻被棄養的小狼當寵物。

在達林太太探索孩子心靈的旅程中，她偶爾會發現一些自己不懂的事物，其中最令她費解的是「彼得潘」三字。

「誰是彼得潘？」她問女兒，「是妳的朋友嗎？」

「媽媽，妳不記得他了？」

達林太太對彼得潘一無所知，但她回想自己的童年後，便想起人們曾說有一位彼得潘與小仙子住在一起。

「就算有這個人，」達林太太對溫蒂說，「他現在也應該長大了。」

「噢，不，他沒有長大。」溫蒂滿懷信心地保證，「他就跟我一樣大。」

「我很擔心彼得潘這個人。」達林太太找丈夫商量，但他只是一笑置之。「聽我的話，」達林先生說，「那只不過是娜娜胡亂告訴他們的，這就是一隻狗會有的念頭。別管它，事情自然就會過去啦。」

但是它並沒有結束。不久之後，這個麻煩的男孩就讓達林太太大吃一驚。

有一天早晨，溫蒂不經意的說出了讓人不安的話。當時，育兒室裡出現了一些樹葉，但孩子們上床時並沒有這些東西，達林太太感到困惑，溫蒂則笑著說：「我相信，一定又是彼得潘幹的好事！」

「溫蒂，妳說的是什麼意思呢？」

「他太頑皮了，也不整理乾淨。」溫蒂嘆了口氣，她一向是個愛乾淨的小孩。

接著，溫蒂坦白地解釋說，彼得潘有時會在晚上來到育兒室，坐在她的床腳，吹

笛子給她聽。

「寶貝，沒有人可以不敲門就進屋子的。」

「我想他是從窗戶進來的吧。」溫蒂說。

「我的天，這裡是三樓啊！妳為什麼不早點告訴我這件事呢？」

「我忘記了。」溫蒂輕聲回答完，便急著吃早餐去了。

但是，無論如何，葉子的確在那裡。達林太太仔細地端詳那些葉子，雖然只剩下葉脈，但她很確定那不是英國境內的樹種。她在房間裡尋找其他線索，但沒有任何發現。

溫蒂一定是在作夢罷了。但翌日晚上發生的事情，證明溫蒂不是在作夢，這晚可以說是這些孩子奇妙冒險的開始呢。

這個夜晚，孩子照例上床睡覺了。娜娜正巧外出不在，達林太太幫孩子梳洗完畢後，就為他們哼唱搖籃曲，直到他們一個接一個鬆開她的手，墜入睡眠的國度。

一切看來如此安適溫暖，達林太太不禁對自己的擔憂感到好笑，她平靜地坐在爐火旁縫衣服。爐火很溫暖，育兒室裡三盞夜燈微弱地亮著，達林太太的膝上放著針線活兒。她打起瞌睡，噢，模樣看來仍十分高雅。

達林太太睡著時作了一個夢。她夢到，有一個奇怪的男孩從一座距離很近的夢幻島中出現。在夢中，他撥開了籠罩夢幻島的濃霧，達林太太看到溫蒂、約翰和麥可從缺口中出現。

這個夢本身應該沒什麼大不了，但達林太太作夢的當兒，育兒室的窗戶被風吹開了，一個男孩跌落到地板上。他的身旁有一個不比拳頭大多少的奇妙光圈，恍若具有生命一般地在房內亂飛亂竄。

達林太太叫了一聲跳起來，看見了那個男孩，她立刻就明白他就是彼得潘。他是一個可愛的男孩，穿著樹葉和藤蔓編織而成的衣裳；最妙的是，他還長著乳牙。他一看見她是個大人，便對著她咬牙切齒，露出一口潔白如珍珠的牙齒。

第二章　影子

達林太太尖叫一聲，宛若是應了鈴響般，房門開了，剛自外頭返家的娜娜衝進來。牠咆哮著撲向男孩，他則輕輕地跳出窗外。達林太太又尖叫一聲，她不希望男孩摔死，於是她跑到屋外尋他的屍體，但卻無所獲。她抬頭看，黑夜裡什麼也看不到，除了一顆她認為是流星的東西。

達林太太回到育兒室，發現娜娜嘴裡含著什麼東西，原來是那個男孩的影子。那孩子往窗外跳時，娜娜很快地關上窗戶，雖然還是來不及捉住他，但他的影子卻來不及離開；窗戶砰地一聲關上，影子被擋住了。

娜娜想將影子掛在窗戶旁，意味著：他一定會回來取走影子，我們把影子放在一個容易取走又不會驚動孩子的地方。但是達林太太覺得那看

起來像是洗滌過的衣物，若是讓鄰居看到的話，達林先生會心煩意亂的。達林太太決定將影子捲起來，小心翼翼地收在抽屜裡，等有適當的時機再轉告丈夫。

一個禮拜後，時機出現了，那是一個讓人絕對忘不了的星期五。

「星期五，我應該要特別謹慎小心的。」達林太太後來一直這樣對丈夫說道，這時，娜娜會在她的身旁握住她的手。

「不，不。」達林先生總是如此說，「我必須負起全部的責任。」

他們就這樣夜復一夜地坐著，回想那個該死的星期五，直到整件事的細節都烙印在腦海中，他們還會從不同的角度再回想一次，好像那件事是一枚有兩個面的劣幣。

「要是我沒有答應參加27號屋的晚宴就好了。」達林太太說。

「要是我不把我的藥水倒進娜娜的碗裡就好了。」達林先生說。

「要是我假裝喜歡喝藥就好了。」這是娜娜濕潤的雙眼想說的。

於是他們一個或不止一個完全崩潰。娜娜心想，「沒錯，沒錯，他們不應該用一隻狗當保姆。」好幾次都是達林先生用手帕為娜娜擦乾眼淚。

他們會坐在空蕩蕩的育兒室，熱切地回憶著那個恐怖的夜晚的一切經過。那個晚上來得很平常，就如同其他數百個夜晚一樣。起初是娜娜為麥可放好洗澡水，駝著他到洗澡間。

隨即，穿著一身雪白晚宴服的達林太太進來了。她今天打扮得稍早了一些，因為溫蒂很喜歡看她穿晚宴服、戴著喬治送的項鍊的模樣。她手上還戴著溫蒂的手鐲，那是她之前跟溫蒂借的，溫蒂很高興能夠將自己的手鐲借給母親。

達林太太看見兩個年長的孩子正在玩耍，扮演丈夫和她在溫蒂出生那天的樣子。

他們繼續回憶。

「然後就是我像旋風一樣地衝進來，對吧？」達林先生會這樣奚落自己；不過，他的確猶如旋風般掃進房裡。

或許，他是情有可原。他也正為宴會打扮，一切都很順利，但等到他拿起領帶後，就不是那麼一回事了。

那天就是這樣。達林先生衝進育兒室，手中抓著一條皺巴巴的領帶。

「天啊，親愛的爸爸，發生什麼事啦？」

「什麼事！」達林先生狂吼，他真的是狂吼。「這條領帶，老是結不上。」他以為達林太太尚未感受到他的怒氣，於是又嚴肅地繼續說，「媽媽，我要警告妳，除非這條領帶能夠在我脖子上打好，否則我們今晚就不去參加晚宴了；假如我今天不去參加晚宴，我就再也不去辦公室上班；假如我再也不去上班，妳跟我就要餓肚子，我們的孩子也要到街上流浪了。」

儘管如此，達林太太仍然很鎮靜。她用冷靜靈巧的雙手為丈夫打上領帶，孩子們則站在一旁靜待命運的宣判。達林太太草草地謝過她，怒氣全消，下一秒鐘他已背著麥可在房裡四處飛舞了。

他們一直玩到娜娜出現為止，不幸的是，達林先生撞到娜娜，褲管沾上了狗毛。那是件新褲子，也是達林先生第一條有穗帶的褲子，達林先生不得不咬住唇，才能忍住眼淚。達林太太立刻為他刷了刷褲子，但他又開始說，讓一隻狗當保姆是個天大的錯誤。

「喬治，娜娜是難得的寶物。」

「這點無庸置疑，但是，我經常感到不安，老覺得牠把孩子當小狗對待。」

「噢不，親愛的，我確定地知道孩子擁有人類的靈魂。」

「我很懷疑，」達林先生深思道，「我很懷疑這一點。」達林太太覺得這是個好時機，可以告訴他彼得潘的事情。起初，達林先生對這個故事嗤之以鼻，但是達林太太拿出影子來時，他開始陷入沉思。

「我不認識這傢伙，」他仔細地檢查影子說，「但看來他不是個好傢伙。」

「妳記得嗎？娜娜拿著麥可的藥水進來時，我們還在討論那個影子。」達林先生說，「娜娜，都是我的錯，害得妳再也不能用嘴銜藥瓶了。」

達林先生儘管強壯，但提到喝藥水，他的行為仍相當幼稚愚蠢。假如他有缺點的話，那就是他一直誤認為自己喝藥時非常勇敢。所以，當麥可開始逃避娜娜嘴裡的藥匙時，達林先生便喝斥道，「麥可，要像個男子漢。」

「不要，不要。」麥可不乖地哭鬧，達林太太只好離開房間去拿塊巧克力哄他，但達林先生認為這顯示麥可不夠堅強。

「媽媽，不要寵壞他，」他在後面喊著，「麥可，我在你的年紀時，喝藥從不抱怨一句。」

他真以為事實就是如此，穿著睡袍的溫蒂也如此深信，所以，為了鼓勵麥可，她說：「爸爸，您常喝的那種藥水更難喝，對不對？」

「難喝多了，」達林先生勇敢地說，「假如我沒把藥瓶搞丟的話，麥可，我現在就會喝給你看。」

他其實並沒有弄丟藥瓶；在一個夜黑風高的晚上，他爬上衣櫃頂，將藥瓶藏在那

15 第一章 影子

裡。但他不知道，忠實的僕人麗莎已經找到了藥瓶，並將它放回臉盆架上。

「爸爸，我知道您的藥瓶在哪裡。」溫蒂大叫，她總是很高興有機會爲他人服務。「我去把它拿來。」達林先生還來不及阻止溫蒂，她就走開了。達林先生的勇氣莫名地消失了。

「約翰，」達林先生打著顫說，「那是世界上最難喝的東西啊。那種藥水又黏又噁心，還甜個半死。」

「一下子就過去了，爸爸。」約翰高興地說，接著就看到溫蒂手拿玻璃藥瓶衝了進來。

「我已經盡量跑快一點了。」她氣喘吁吁地說。

「妳的速度還真驚人。」達林先生回答，帶著一種報復性的禮貌斥責她。「麥可先喝。」他推託說。

「爸爸先。」天性多疑的麥可說。

「你知道，我應該要生病才喝藥的。」達林先生語帶威脅地說。

溫蒂相當困惑地說：「爸爸，我以爲您能很簡單地解決它的。」

「這不是重點。」達林先生回嘴，「重點是，我瓶裡的藥水比麥可湯匙裡的還多。」他驕傲的自尊近乎消失殆盡。

「爸爸，我在等您喝藥呢。」麥可冷酷地說。

「你倒說得好，你在等我喝；我也在等著你喝呢。」溫蒂心生一計，她說：「你們何不同時喝呢？」

「當然好，」達林先生說，「準備好了嗎，麥可？」

溫蒂數著，一、二、三，麥可吞下藥水，但達林先生迅速將藥瓶藏到身後。

麥可發出怒吼，溫蒂則尖叫起來：「噢，爸爸！」

三個孩子看著他的眼神相當令人畏懼，似乎他們已經不再尊敬他了。「你們聽我說。」達林先生哀求地說，娜娜這時正好跑到浴室去，「我想到一個好主意，我把藥水倒入娜娜的碗裡，這樣牠就會誤當是牛奶喝下去。」

藥水的顏色和牛奶的一樣。不過，這些孩子可沒有父親的幽默感，他們都以譴責的眼神看著父親將藥倒入娜娜碗裡。「多麼有趣啊。」達林先生不太有信心地說。達林太太與娜娜回來了，但這些孩子不敢揭發父親的行為。

「娜娜，好狗兒。」達林先生拍拍娜娜，「我在你的碗裡倒了牛奶囉，娜娜。」

娜娜搖搖尾巴，衝到碗旁，開始舔起藥來。牠看了達林先生一眼，眼裡並沒有生氣的神情，只是從通紅的眼裡溢出了斗大的眼淚，接著，牠便拖著腳爬回狗窩。

達林先生感到極度羞愧，但他並不肯認輸。在一片可怕的靜默中，達林太太聞了聞娜娜的碗。

「噢，喬治，」她叫道，「這是你的藥哪！」

「只是開個小玩笑。」達林先生吼道。達林太太安撫兩個男孩，溫蒂摟著娜娜。

「太好了。」他沉痛地說：「我只是想試著讓這個家有趣一點，卻害我萬夫所指。」

溫蒂仍然抱著娜娜。「很好。」達林先生又吼叫道，「把娜娜寵壞吧！都沒人來寵我。我只是一個賺錢養家的工具！」

「喬治，」達林太太責備他，「別這麼大聲，僕人們會聽到的。」他們喜歡把麗莎一個人叫做僕人們。

「就讓他們聽吧！」他狂暴地答道，「讓全世界都聽見也無所謂。但我就是不要再讓那隻狗稱霸這間育兒室了。」

孩子開始哭泣，娜娜跑到達林先生面前求情，但他揮手要牠回去。他覺得自己又變成一個強大的男人了。「沒有用的，沒有用的。」他嚷道，「適合妳的地方是庭院，妳這個時間應該被綁在那裡才對。」

「喬治，喬治，」達林太太低聲說，「別忘了我跟你提過的彼得潘。」

第一章 影子

但是達林先生才聽不下去呢！他要顯示自己才是這個家的主人，所以將娜娜拖了出去。

同時，在罕見的沉默氣氛中，達林太太讓孩子們上了床，並點亮夜燈。他們可以聽到娜娜正在外頭吠叫，約翰嗚咽地說，「都是爸爸把牠綁在院子裡。」

溫蒂比較懂事，「那不是娜娜難過的叫聲，」溫蒂說，「那是牠嗅到危險靠近時的叫聲。」

危險！

「溫蒂，妳確定？」

「喔，是的。」

達林太太全身發顫，她走到了窗邊，窗戶已關緊了。她向外看，漆黑的夜空中佈滿星星。儘管麥可已半睡，他也察覺到了母親的不安，他問道：「媽媽，夜燈亮了之後，會有東西來傷害我們嗎？」

「不會，寶貝，」達林太太回答，「夜燈就是媽媽留下的眼睛，幫助她守護她的寶貝。」

她走到各個床前為孩子哼唱催眠歌。小麥可伸出雙手抱住她說：「媽媽，我真高興有妳。」這是很久以前達林太太聽到小麥可所說的最後一句話。

27號屋子距達林家只有幾碼遠，但是地面已經積了點雪，所以達林夫婦繞著路走，以免弄髒自己的鞋。街上的行人只剩他們兩個，滿天的星星都俯瞰著他們。當達林夫婦到達目的地，27號的門一關上時，天空中立刻出現了一陣騷動，銀河裡所有的小星星幾乎是異口同聲地叫道：「就是現在，彼得潘！」

第三章　走吧，走吧！

達林夫婦離家後，孩子床邊的三盞夜燈仍然明亮地燃著。但不久，溫蒂床旁的夜燈眨了眨眼，打了一個大呵欠，使得另外兩盞燈也跟著打起呵欠，嘴巴都還沒來得及闔上，三盞燈就都熄滅了。

現在，房裡出現了另一道光，比那些夜燈亮了幾千倍。它其實不是一道光，而是一位仙子，不比你的手掌大。這位仙子名叫叮噹貝爾，身上穿著薄葉製成的衣裳，十分精緻，又短又窄，展露出她體型上的優點。她有點兒豐滿。

仙子進來沒有多久，窗戶便被小星星的呼氣吹開，彼得潘進來了。

彼得潘輕聲喚道，「叮噹，妳在哪裡？」叮噹正待在一個水壺裡，她十分喜歡那個地方，她從未待在水壺裡呢。

「哎呀，快從水壺裡出來吧，告訴我，妳知道他們把我的影子藏在哪裡嗎？」

如銀鈴所發出的可愛叮噹聲回答了彼得潘的話。這是仙子的語言。

叮噹說影子放在抽屜，於是彼得潘跳向抽屜，把抽屜裡的東西倒落一地，一下子就找到自己的影子。他太高興了，竟不小心把叮噹貝爾關在抽屜裡。

如果彼得潘也會思考他一定認為，他的影子一挨進他，就會像雨滴水珠般融合在一起。所以當結果不如預期時，他不禁大驚失色。他試著用浴室拿來的泡沫將影子黏上，但是無效。彼得潘打了一陣寒顫，他跌坐地板上，哭了起來。

他的啜泣聲吵醒了溫蒂，她在床上坐起身來。

「男孩，」她禮貌地問，「你爲什麼哭呢？」

彼得潘也很有禮貌，他曾在仙子的盛會中學會莊重的禮儀；他站起身，優雅地向溫蒂鞠躬。溫蒂很高興，也在床上回禮。

「妳叫什麼名字？」彼得潘問道。

「溫蒂・摩羅・安琪拉・達林，」溫蒂得意地回答，「你呢？」

「彼得潘。」

溫蒂問他住在什麼地方。

「第二個圈圈向右轉，」彼得潘說，「然後直走，一直走到清晨。」

「這地址真怪！」

彼得潘感到喪氣，第一次覺得自己的地址可能很怪。「不，並不怪。」他說。

「我的意思是，」溫蒂想起自己是主人，便親切地回答，「信件上面寫的地址也是這樣嗎？」

他真希望她沒提起信件這種東西。「我沒有信。」彼得潘傲慢地回答。

「但你母親總會收到信吧？」

「我沒有母親。」他說。他不但沒有母親，也壓根兒沒想到要有母親，他覺得母親是種很討人厭的人。溫蒂覺得出現在自己眼前的是個悲劇人物。

「噢，彼得潘，難怪你在哭。」她一邊說著，一邊爬下床跑向他。

「我並不是因為沒有母親而哭，」彼得潘相當憤怒地說，「我哭是因為我的影子黏不回去。妳有辦法黏回去嗎？」

溫蒂忍不住微笑。**真是個小孩子！**

幸好，她立刻就知道該怎麼辦。「這要用縫的才行。」溫蒂有點兒自負地說。

「我得說這會有點痛。」溫蒂警告彼得潘。

「喔，我不會哭的。」彼得潘說，自以為一生從未哭過。他咬緊牙關，並沒有哭。很快地，影子又回到了原來的位置，不過還是有點兒皺痕。

「或許我應該把它燙平。」溫蒂體貼地說。但孩子氣的彼得潘對自己的外表漠不關心,他此刻已開心得蹦蹦跳跳了。天啊,他已經忘記這份喜悅得歸功於溫蒂了,他還以為是自己把影子黏好的呢。「我多麼聰明啊。」他狂喜地歡呼。

雖然這麼說有點兒難堪,但彼得潘這種自負的個性正是他迷人的特質之一。

不過,溫蒂有一瞬間嚇到了。「你這自負的孩子,」她挖苦地說,「當然囉,我什麼忙都沒幫上!」

「妳的確幫了一點小忙。」彼得潘不經意地說,繼續跳著舞。

「一點小忙!」溫蒂高傲地回答,「如果我沒派上用場,那我引退好了。」接著她便以莊嚴的姿態衝回床上,用毛毯蒙住自己的臉。

彼得潘為了讓溫蒂伸出頭來,便假裝要離開。這個方法失敗後,他在溫蒂的床尾坐了下來,用腳輕輕地踢她。「溫蒂,」彼得潘繼續說,那種聲音實在沒有一個女人可以抗拒,「溫蒂,其實,一個女孩子比二十個男孩子有用多了。」

「你真的這麼想嗎?彼得潘?」

「嗯,是的。」

溫蒂說,如果彼得潘願意的話,她可以給他一個吻,但他不懂她的意思,竟期待地伸出手來。

「你真的知道吻是什麼嗎？」溫蒂嚇了一跳。

「妳給我一個吻的時候，我就知道了。」彼得潘笨拙地回答。為了不要讓他傷心，溫蒂在他手中放了一個頂針。

「現在，」彼得潘說，「我也該回妳一個吻嗎？」溫蒂矜持地答道：「假如你願意。」她輕浮地把臉靠向彼得潘，但是他只是將一個橡樹果實放到她手裡。溫蒂只好緩緩地縮回臉，親切地說她會將他的吻掛在頸鏈上。

彼此介紹過之後，照例會再詢問對方年齡，做事喜歡照規矩來的溫蒂便問彼得潘幾歲了。

「我不知道，」彼得潘不安地回答，他有點兒疑慮，但還是冒昧的說：「溫蒂，我在出生的那一天就逃跑了。」

「為什麼呢？」溫蒂問道。

「我根本就不想長大。」他憤慨地說，「我想要永遠當個小孩，四處遊玩。所以我逃到肯辛頓花園，和仙子們住了好長一段時間。」

「仙子？」溫蒂睜大眼睛吸了口氣。他告訴了溫蒂關於仙子的誕生

「溫蒂，妳知道仙子嗎？初生的寶寶第一次笑的時候，笑聲會碎成一千片，一片一片四處跳躍，這就是仙子的誕生。」

儘管這番談話很冗長，但甚少外出的溫蒂仍聽得津津有味。

「而且，」彼得潘繼續溫柔地說，「每個男孩女孩都應該有一個守護仙子。」

「應該有？現在沒有了嗎？」

「沒有了。你知道，現在的孩子懂得好多事，很快就不再相信仙子的故事了。每次一有孩子說『我才不相信仙子』，就會有一個仙子在什麼地方墜落而死。」

彼得潘認為關於仙子的事情已說得夠多了，他也很驚訝叮噹貝爾一直沒有任何動靜。「我不知道她到哪裡去了。」他說著，站起身來呼喚叮噹的名字。溫蒂興奮地顫抖，心撲撲地跳了起來。

「彼得潘，」溫蒂捉住彼得潘叫道，「你可沒告訴我房裡有位仙子呢！」

「她剛剛還在這裡，」他有點不耐煩的回答，「妳聽見她的聲音了嗎？」他們一起豎起耳朵聽。

「我只聽到一種聲音，」溫蒂說，「像是鈴鐺響的叮噹聲。」

聲音從抽屜傳出來，彼得潘臉上露出了快樂的神色。

「溫蒂，」彼得潘高興地低聲說，「我相信我是把她關在抽屜裡了。」

他將可憐的叮噹從抽屜裡放了出來，她氣憤地在育兒室裡邊飛邊叫。

溫蒂並沒有聽他說話。「噢，彼得潘，」她叫道，「她能不能停住不動，讓我好好瞧瞧！」

「仙子很少會停下來的。」彼得潘回答，但是溫蒂猛然看到那奇幻浪漫的身影停在布穀鳥時鐘上休息。「喔，真可愛啊！」溫蒂嚷道，儘管叮噹仍然一臉憤怒。

「叮噹，」彼得潘溫柔地說，「這位小淑女說，她希望妳做她的仙子。」

叮噹的回答相當無禮傲慢。

「她不過是個很普通的仙子，」彼得潘帶著歉意解釋，「她叫叮噹貝爾，專門負責補鍋子。」

他們倆個現在一起坐在大靠椅上，溫蒂又向彼得潘追問更多問題。他告訴他有關於失蹤的男孩，他們是嬰兒時期跌出嬰兒車的孩子。

「我是他們的隊長。」

「好有趣喔！但是那裡沒有女孩啊？」

「噢，沒有。妳知道的，女生都很聰明，她們才不會掉出嬰兒車呢。」

「說得真好！所以你可以給我一個頂針。」溫蒂臉紅著說道。

突然間，溫蒂尖叫一聲，彷彿有人拉了她頭髮。

「一定是叮噹搞得鬼，我從沒見她這麼調皮過。」

的確，叮噹又開始四處飛舞，同時口出攻擊的話。

「溫蒂，她說只要我給妳頂針，她就會這麼對妳。」

「為什麼？」

「叮噹，為什麼？」

叮噹又回答了同樣的話：「你這個愚蠢的笨蛋。」彼得潘不懂到底是什麼原因，但溫蒂已經明白。當彼得潘坦承自己來育兒室的窗口是為了聽故事而非來看她時，溫蒂覺得有點兒沮喪。

「妳知道燕子為什麼選在屋簷築巢嗎？就是因為牠們想聽故事啊。喔，溫蒂，妳母親跟妳講了一個有趣的故事。」

「哪一個故事？」

「一個王子找不到穿玻璃鞋女孩的故事。」

「彼得潘，」溫蒂興奮地說，「那是灰姑娘，王子後來找到她了，他們從此過著幸福快樂的日子。」

彼得潘高興地從地板上站起來，急急忙忙地走向窗戶。「你要去哪裡？」溫蒂疑惑地問道。

「去告訴那些男孩故事的結局。」

「不要走，彼得潘，」溫蒂懇求道，「我還有好多故事可以講給你聽。」

「溫蒂，跟我一起走，說故事給其他男孩聽。」

溫蒂當然很高興彼得潘的邀請，但她回答：「噢，親愛的，我不能去，我得顧慮到我的母親！況且，我也不會飛。」

「我可以教妳。」

「噢，飛翔會多麼美妙啊。」

「我會教妳如何乘上風兒的背脊，這樣我們就能走了。」

「哇啊！」溫蒂歡喜地嚷嚷。

「想想那些迷路的男孩會有多愛妳，」彼得潘繼續說道，「晚上時，妳還可以把

　第二章　走吧，走吧！

我們一個一個塞進睡袋。」

「妳還可以幫我們補衣服、縫口袋。我們的衣服都沒有口袋。」

溫蒂無法抗拒了。「這真的相當誘人！」她叫道，「彼得潘，你也能教約翰及麥可飛行嗎？」

「如果妳希望。」彼得潘淡淡地說。於是，溫蒂跑向約翰及麥可，搖醒他們。

「醒一醒，」她叫道，「彼得潘來了，他要教我們飛呢。」

約翰揉揉雙眼回答：「那麼我就起床。」這時候麥可也起來了。

突然間，彼得潘轉過身來示意「噓！」。四周一片寂靜，一切都很正常。娜娜整個晚上都難過地吠個不停，但現在卻變安靜了。他們聽到了娜娜的沉默。

「熄燈！躲起來！快點！」約翰指揮大家。

麗莎拉著娜娜進來時，育兒室已恢復了往常的昏暗平靜，你還可以聽到了三個淘氣的小傢伙睡著時可愛的呼吸聲。其實，他們正躲在窗簾後面假裝打鼾呢。

「瞧，妳這個多疑的畜生。」麗莎斥道，絲毫不給娜娜面子。「他們都好端端的，不是嗎？」

娜娜分辨得出來那種呼吸聲不太對勁，於是牠努力地想掙脫麗莎的掌控。可惜，麗莎很駑鈍。「夠了，娜娜。」她堅決地說，硬是把娜娜拖離房間。

麗莎重新綁住悲傷的狗兒。娜娜眼見無法得到麗莎的協助，便竭力掙扎，終於把鏈條給弄斷。一眨眼工夫，牠就已經衝到27號屋子的晚宴廳裡，舉起腳掌朝天晃動，這是牠最有效的溝通方式。達林夫婦立刻明白育兒室裡一定出了事情，他們來不及向主人辭別，就立刻衝到街上了。

「沒事了。」約翰從躲藏的地方現身宣佈道。「彼得潘，我想問你，你真的能飛嗎？」

彼得潘並沒有多做麻煩的回答，只在房裡飛了一圈，半途還拾起壁爐架。

飛翔看來很簡單，溫蒂他們三人先站在地板上試，接著又到床上試，但卻都飛不上去，反而跌了下來。

無疑地，彼得潘只是在開他們玩笑，除非身上灑有仙塵，否則誰都飛不起來。彼得潘一隻手上沾滿了仙塵，所以他在孩子身上吹了一些，便產生了絕妙的效果。

「現在，像這樣動動你們的肩膀，」彼得潘說，「然後往上飛。」

三個孩子都站在床上，勇敢的麥可率先飛起來。他其實不是真的有意要飛，但才一試，他就飛越整個房間。

他們飛翔的動作沒有彼得潘靈活優美，兩隻腿仍會亂踢，不過還是都可以飛到頭頂上了天花板，這實在太妙不可言了。

「嘿，」約翰叫道，「我們為什麼不飛出去呢？」

這正是彼得潘引誘他們的目的。

這個時候，達林夫婦已隨著娜娜離開了27號房。他們跑到街上，望著育兒室的窗戶；沒錯，育兒室的門仍關著，但燈火通明，最讓人驚詫的是，從窗簾上可以看見三個穿著夜袍的人影在屋裡轉來轉去，不是在地板上，是在半空中。

不，不是三個身影，是四個！

他們顫抖著身子，打開了大門。達林先生本來要衝上樓，但達林太太示意他放輕腳步，甚至試著想讓自己的心情平靜一點。

若是天空中的小星星沒瞧見他們，他們應該是可以及時趕到育兒室的。因為繁星這回又把窗戶吹開，最小的那顆星喊道：「彼得潘，小心！」

彼得潘知道他們不能再耽擱了。「來吧。」他霸道地叫道，立刻飛入黑夜中，約翰、麥可和溫蒂尾隨著他飛了起來。

達林夫婦跟娜娜衝到育兒室時，為時已晚了。

◥ 第二章　走吧，走吧！

第四章　飛航

「第二個圈圈向右轉，然後一直走到天亮。」

彼得潘之前告訴溫蒂，說這就是到夢幻島的途徑。但單憑著這句話，就算是讓小鳥帶著地圖查看，牠們恐怕也到不了夢幻島。溫蒂、約翰與麥可沒有別的選擇，只能完全信任地跟著彼得潘。

他帶領著他們繞著教堂的尖頂，鐘樓或者其他高大的建築物飛舞。

天色時暗時亮，天氣也忽冷忽熱。他們追逐小鳥，搶奪牠們口中適合人類吃的食物，然後鳥兒也會追著他們搶回食物，他們就這樣快樂地互相追逐了好幾哩，在雙方互相釋出善意後，才分道揚鑣。

他們現在飛得還不錯，雖然有時雙腿還是會蹬到，但至少已經飛的很平穩了。

彼得潘偶爾會脫隊，害獨自飛行的他們覺得很寂寞。彼得潘飛的速度比他們快多了，所以他有時會突然不見蹤影，跑去加入一場他們無法參與的冒險。彼得潘會狂

第四章　飛航

笑的飛下來，因為他向一顆星星說了笑話，但是他已忘了說的是什麼；有時他又飛上來，身上還黏著美人魚的鱗片，但又說不出究竟遇到了什麼事。

彼得潘最後還是會回來，但有時候他似乎不記得他們了，像是準備下一次的冒險。有一次溫蒂甚至要說出自己的名字。

「我是溫蒂。」她激動地說。

彼得潘感到很抱歉。「溫蒂，」他低聲對她說，「如果妳看見我忘記妳了，妳只要一直說『我是溫蒂』，那我就會記起來了。」

當然這不大令人滿意。彼得潘為了彌補這個遺憾，便教他們如何仰臥在強勁的順風上，他們嘗試了好幾遍，發現就此可以安穩地睡覺後，高興得不得了。

過了好幾個月之後，他們真的到達夢幻島了。他們筆直的朝島嶼飛過去，這或許不能說是彼得潘或叮噹帶路帶得好，而該說是那座島也正在眺望他們。

溫蒂、約翰和麥可三人在空中踮起腳尖望著夢幻島。說也奇怪，他們立刻就認識這個地方，在還沒有開始害怕之前，他們先向夢幻島歡呼，他們不把夢幻島當夢想已久而終於看到的東西，而是當做度假回家見到了老朋友一樣。

天色漸漸變暗，四周也沒有夜燈，娜娜也不在身邊保護他們的安全。孩子們此刻只能依靠自己。

他們之前本來是飛散的，但現在全都緊湊到彼得潘身旁。他們正在一座可怕的島嶼上空，飛行高度不高，有時還會有樹木勾到他們的腳。空氣中其實看不到什麼恐怖的事物，但他們前進的速度變得相當緩慢且吃力，宛如正在敵軍之間殺出一條路。

「他們不希望我們降落。」彼得潘解釋。

「他們是誰？」溫蒂發著抖低聲問。

但彼得潘不能說，也不願說。叮噹貝爾早已在他的肩頭上睡著了，彼得潘叫醒她，要她去前方探路。

有時，彼得潘會停在空中，手圈在耳朵旁專心傾聽，然後再向下注視，銳利的目光恍若會將地面穿出兩個洞似的。之後，他才會再度往前飛。

彼得潘的勇氣幾乎有點過頭了。「你想要先去冒險？」他很不經意地問約翰，

「還是想先喝杯茶？」

「哪一類的冒險？」約翰小心地問道。

「在我們下方的大草原上，有一個海盜正熟睡著呢，」彼得潘回答，「如果你願

意的話，我們就飛下去殺了他。」

「萬一，」約翰啞著聲音說，「他正好醒了過來呢？」

彼得潘憤怒地說：「你該不會以為我要趁他睡覺時動手吧！我會先把他叫醒，再殺了他，我一向這麼辦事的。」

雖然約翰口中嘆著「多棒啊」，他還是決定要先喝茶。他問彼得潘島上現在是否有很多海盜，彼得潘回答說，他從來沒見過那麼多海盜出現在這裡。

「現在誰是船長？」

「虎克。」彼得潘回答。他在說這幾個討厭的字時，臉上的神情變得很難看。

「詹姆斯·虎克？」

麥可開始哭了，連約翰都哽咽起來，他們都聽過惡名昭彰的虎克。

「虎克不像以前那麼巨大了，我削掉他的右手。」彼得潘繼續道，「假如我們與虎克對戰，你必須將他留給我對付。」

「我答應你。」約翰由衷地答道。

此刻，他們又稍微放心了一點，因為叮噹已飛回他們身邊，有了叮噹的光芒，他們能夠很清楚地看到彼此。遺憾的是，叮噹的速度慢不下來，所以她只好繞著他們不停地打轉，使他們就像在光圈中移動一般。溫蒂原本很喜歡這樣，但後來彼得潘指出了問題。叮噹的光芒可能讓海盜更容易看到他們。

「彼得潘，叫叮噹立刻走開。」三個小孩異口同聲要求，但是彼得潘拒絕了。

「叮噹覺得我們已經迷路了。」彼得潘頑固地回答，「而且她很害怕。你們別想要我在她害怕時，把她打發走！」

光圈的光芒霎時間滅了，彼得潘覺得有東西親暱地摟了他一把。

「你告訴她，」溫蒂哀求，「把光熄掉吧。」

「她沒有辦法停止發光，這可能是仙子唯一辦不到的事情，只有在她睡著時，她的光芒才會自動熄滅，就跟星星一樣。」

彼得潘忽然有了一個好主意。**約翰的帽子！**

叮噹說，如果他們把帽子拿在手上的話，她就同意躲在帽子裡。儘管她比較希望帽子由彼得潘拿著，但後來卻由約翰負責。又因為約翰抱怨帽子會撞到他的膝蓋，所以就換成溫蒂拿。

黑色的帽子完全遮蓋住叮噹的光芒，他們一行人默默地往前飛。那種沉默的氣氛前所未見，偶爾，遠處會傳來波浪輕擊的聲音和像是樹枝互相摩擦的沙沙聲，彼得潘卻解釋說那是動物舔水的聲音和印地安人磨刀霍霍的聲音。

最後，連這些聲音都不見了。對麥可而言，這種沉寂相當恐怖。「拜託，來點聲音吧！」他大聲說。

好像是應他請求似的，空氣中傳來一聲前所未聞的轟隆巨響——海盜開始朝他們發射長程炮了。

三個驚慌的孩子此時深刻地體會到，虛構的島嶼和真實的島嶼有多大的差異。

天空再度恢復平靜時，約翰和麥可發現黑暗中只剩他們兩人。約翰無意識地蹬著空氣，原本不懂得漂浮的麥可此時竟漂浮在空中。

「你中槍了嗎？」約翰驚恐地低聲問道。

「沒有。」麥可悄聲回答。

彼得潘被一陣風遠遠地吹到了海面上，溫蒂則被吹到高處，身旁只剩下叮噹。

叮噹並沒有那麼壞，只是仙子的身體很小，所以在一段時間內只能容下一種情感。此刻，叮噹非常忌妒溫蒂。看到有個機會可以擺脫溫蒂，叮噹指示女孩跟著她。

她並不知道叮噹對她充滿了女人的忌妒，心慌意亂的溫蒂只好搖搖晃晃地跟著叮噹，飛向她的宿命。

第五章　成真的島嶼

察覺到彼得潘已在回來的路上，夢幻島又醒過來了。

彼得潘不在時，島上經常是一片靜悄悄。仙子清晨休息的時間變長了，野獸專心照顧幼獸，印地安人連著六天六夜大吃大喝，連海盜跟迷路的孩子相遇時，也只會對彼此咬咬大拇指示威而已。

這個夜晚，島上各個主要勢力的活動如下：迷路的男孩們正在尋找彼得潘，海盜正在尋找迷路的孩子，印地安人正在尋找海盜，野獸則在尋找印地安人。他們沿著島環繞，不過因為他們走的速率是一樣的，所以都沒有碰頭。

第一個經過的是托托，在這群勇敢的隊伍裡，他絕對不是最膽小的，卻是運氣最差的。這種霉運使他臉露愁容，不過他的脾氣並沒有因此變壞，反而是變好了，他是最謙遜的一個男孩。

接著走過來的是活潑開朗的尼伯斯，後面跟著的是史萊特利，他正吹著用樹枝製成的笛子，照著自己的調子忘我地跳舞呢；史萊特利是最愛裝腔作勢的一個孩子。搗蛋鬼柯利排在第四個，每當彼得潘板著臉問「誰做的？站起來」，十次有九次都是他自首出列；後來，無論是不是他的錯，只要聽到這個命令他就會自動站起來。最後過來的是一對雙胞胎，因為我們弄不清楚誰是誰，也就無法形容他們。

這些男孩在夜色中消失了，過了一會兒，不過也沒多久，因為這個島上的步驟很快，海盜的隊伍出現了。還沒見到他們之前，我們就聽到了他們的歌聲，老是唱著一首駭人的歌曲。

走在這幫海盜最前面的是英俊的義大利人西柯，他曾在監獄獄長的背上刻下自己的名字；後面跟著渾身刺青的比爾喬克。接下來的是庫克森與史塔克紳士，史塔克是裡面最有禮貌的，他曾經在學校當助教員，對殺人的手法有其堅持。還有愛爾蘭籍的海盜史密、努得，以及其他的惡棍。

在他們之間，最邪惡也最重要的人物，非詹姆斯‧虎克莫屬。虎克的臉暗沉黝黑，滿頭捲捲的黑髮；他一雙承滿憂鬱的藍眼眸教人難忘，但在他舉起鐵鉤刺向你時，雙瞳就會變得血紅，駭人地亮了起來⋯⋯他的談吐非常優雅，就算是在賭咒時亦不例外，動作也很高貴，這一切都使他跟其他海盜看來明顯不同。據說，這個天不怕地不怕的男人唯一害怕的，就是看到自己的血，他的血很濃而且顏色異常。

跟在海盜隊伍後面的是印第安人。他們像影子般潛行，手持戰斧和刀劍。其中包括美麗的印地安公主「老虎莉莉」，她驕傲的挺著身子，露出應有的公主風範。

而在印第安人後面的是一群野獸：獅子、老虎、熊，還有許多見了他們就逃開的小野獸。

牠們經過後，最後出現的是一隻巨大無比的鱷魚。

鱷魚經過後不久，迷路的孩子們又出現了。這個循環會如此不停地持續下去，除非其中有一隊人馬駐足或改變行進速度，到那個時候，牠們就會開始起衝突。

第一個脫離這個循環的是迷路的男孩們，他們撲倒在地底之家附近的草皮上。

「我真希望彼得潘已經回來了，然後告訴我們更多關於玻璃鞋女孩的故事。」史萊特利說。

他們談起灰姑娘仙杜瑞拉，托托充滿自信地說，他的母親一定很像仙杜瑞拉。只有在彼得潘不在時，他們才能提到母親，因為彼得潘認為這個話題很愚蠢，禁止他們談論。突然間男孩們停下，因為海盜們正在接近。

除了尼伯斯留下來偵查之外，其他人都已經回到地底下的家了。不過，孩子們又是怎麼到家的？地面上根本看不見入口，也沒有被一堆木柴祕密掩蓋起來的洞穴啊。

不過，請仔細地瞧，你會發現附近有七株大樹，每棵樹的樹幹都是空心的，樹上面都有一個正好符合男孩身材的樹洞。這就是通往地底之家的入口。

海盜走近了，史塔克的眼快，瞧見尼伯斯逃進樹林中，他立刻開了一槍。但是，一隻鐵爪搭上他的肩頭。

「饒了我，船長。」史塔克一邊掙扎一邊尖叫。

虎克威脅地說：「先把槍收起來。」

「那是你討厭的男孩，我本來可以殺死他的。」

「史密，現在不是時候。」虎克凶狠地說，「那只不過是一個，我想要的是一次解決全部七個男孩。現在我們大家分散去找他們。」

海盜分頭走入樹林，瞬間只剩下虎克船長和史密。虎克重重地嘆了一口氣。

「最重要的是，」虎克激動地說道，「我要捉到他們的首領彼得潘，那個砍掉我手臂的傢伙。」他威嚇地揮舞他的鐵鉤。「我等著用這個鐵鉤跟他握手等好久了，噢，我要把他撕了。」

第五章 成眞的島嶼

「彼得潘把我的手拉到一隻恰好經過的鱷魚口中。」虎克有點畏縮地說道。

「難怪我常覺得，」史密說，「你對鱷魚有種莫名的恐懼。」

「不是對所有的鱷魚，」虎克糾正史密，「我怕的只有那一隻鱷魚。」他放低聲音：「史密，那隻鱷魚很喜歡吃我的手臂，所以自那時開始，牠就一直跟著我，不管是上山或下海，一看見我這個殘剩的身體，便饞得張大嘴巴。」

虎克在一株大蘑菇上坐了下來，聲音開始有一點兒發抖。「史密，」他粗聲的說，「那隻鱷魚本來早就要把我吃掉了，幸虧牠吞下了一座鐘，在牠的體內滴答滴答地響，所以只要牠一靠近，我就可以聽到滴答滴答的聲音，好趕快逃跑。」他笑了，但卻是乾笑。

「有一天，」史密說，「鬧鐘的電池會用盡，那牠就會抓到你了。」

虎克潤了潤乾燥的唇。「是啊，」他說，「我怕的就是這個。」

打從一坐下來，虎克就奇怪地感覺暖和起來。「史密，」他說，「這個位置好熱。」

於是，他們開始研究這個蘑菇，發現它的硬度和大小是這島上所不曾見過的。

他們試著想把蘑菇拔起來，竟然一下子就拔起來了，因為那個蘑菇根本就沒有長根。

更奇怪的是，蘑菇拔起來後，還有一縷煙冉冉上升，兩個海盜彼此對看。「一根煙囪！」他們異口同聲叫道。

傳出來的不只有煙霧，還有孩童的聲音，這些男孩們覺得他們的藏身之地十分安全，所以就肆無忌憚地聊天。海盜陰險地聽了一會兒後，就把蘑菇放回原位。他們向四周望了望，就發現了七棵樹上的洞。

「你有聽到他們說彼得潘不在家嗎？」史密輕聲說道，急著想讓他的強尼螺絲栓派上用場。

虎克點點頭。他站著沉思了半晌，終於，他黝黑的臉龐上出現一抹冷笑。

「回到船上去，」虎克說著，「烤一塊厚厚的蛋糕，上面要淋滿綠綠的糖漿。我們把蛋糕放在有美人魚的珊瑚湖湖沿岸，這些男孩經常會到那裡游泳，跟美人魚玩耍，他們看到蛋糕一定會狼吞虎嚥地吃下去，因為，沒有母親的孩子不會知道撿起好吃的蛋糕來吃有多危險。」虎克船長大笑，這回不是乾笑，而是真笑。

他們開始唱起歌來，但卻沒有唱完，因為有另一個聲音出現，使他們不敢作聲──

滴答滴答滴答滴答！

虎克全身打顫，一隻腳揚在空中。

「是那隻鱷魚。」他喘息說著便轉身逃走，他身旁的海盜們也跟著逃走。

男孩們又到地面上來了，突然尼伯斯在天空中看到了一些東西。

「我看到了一樣奇妙的東西。」尼伯斯嚷起來，其他人急急地圍到他身旁。「有一隻好大的白鳥正朝我們這裡飛過來。」

「你認為那是什麼鳥？」

「我不知道，」尼伯斯帶著敬畏回答，「但是牠看起來很疲憊，邊飛邊嘆氣說：

『可憐的溫蒂。』」

溫蒂現在差不多就在這群男孩的頭頂上空，他們還可以聽到她悲哀的叫聲，叮噹貝爾尖銳的聲音更是清晰可聞。這個妒火中燒的仙子現在已經卸下友誼的面具，從各個角度襲擊溫蒂，野蠻地撞著她的肉。

「嗨，叮噹。」這群吃驚的男孩叫道。

叮噹的回答傳來：「彼得潘要你們殺了溫蒂。」

「快點，托托，快點，」叮噹叫道，「彼得潘會很高興的。」

托托興奮地搭箭上弓。「叮噹，走開。」他吼道，隨後射出箭。溫蒂的胸口被一根箭刺到了，飄飄搖搖地墜落下來。

第六章 小屋

「我射中溫蒂啦！」托托驕傲地說，「彼得潘一定會以我為榮。」

他們全都聚集在溫蒂身旁定睛看著，此時的氣氛靜得可怕，如果溫蒂的心臟還在跳動，他們應該都聽得到。

史萊特利首先發言。「這不是鳥，」他驚恐地說道，「我想，這是個女孩子。」

「依我看來，」柯利說，「她應該是彼得潘帶來的。」他哀傷地撲倒在地。

「是我的錯。」托托懺悔地說，他緩緩地走開。

「別走。」其他的男孩都憐憫地叫了起來。

「我必須走，」托托發著抖說，「我怕彼得潘。」

在這個悲傷的時刻，一個聲音出現了，他們全都大吃一驚，他們聽到了彼得潘的歡呼聲。

「哈囉，男孩。」彼得潘大聲招呼，男孩們機械性地行禮，接著又是一陣沉默。

彼得潘皺起眉頭。

男孩們張開嘴，卻發不出歡呼聲。不過，彼得潘急著想告訴他們好消息，所以就該往這邊飛來了。」

饒了他們。

「孩子，我有個好消息，」彼得潘叫道，「我為你們找來了一個母親。我想她應該往這邊飛來了。」

所以，其他男孩都讓開了。彼得潘見到了溫蒂，他楞了一會兒，也不知該怎麼辦才好。那裡有一隻箭。他將箭從溫蒂胸口拔了出來，望向其他人。

托托命令道：「雙胞胎，退後，讓彼得潘知道真相吧。」

「誰的箭？」他厲聲追問。

「彼得潘，是我的。」托托跪了下來，說道。

「天啊，你這卑鄙的傢伙。」彼得潘說著，舉起弓箭想當作刀子。

彼得潘兩次舉起箭來，但兩次都放了手。「我沒辦法真的刺你，」他敬畏地說，

「好像有什麼東西在拉著我的手。」

所有人都驚訝地望向彼得潘，只有尼伯斯例外，他恰好看著溫蒂。

「是溫蒂，」尼伯斯叫了起來，「瞧，是她的手。」

「她還活著。」彼得潘簡短地說道。

史萊特利立刻嚷嚷：「溫蒂小姐還活著。」

於是彼得潘在溫蒂身旁跪了下來，他發現了自己的鈕扣。當時溫蒂將彼得潘的橡樹果實鈕釦繫在頸鍊上。

「瞧，」彼得潘說，「箭射中了這個玩意兒。這是我給她的吻，救了她的命。」

「我記得吻是什麼，」史萊特利插嘴說，「讓我瞧瞧。嗯，的確是個吻。」

彼得潘並沒有聽他說話，他正哀求溫蒂快點好起來，如此才能帶她去看美人魚。

當然，溫蒂仍很虛弱，沒辦法回答他。此時，天空中傳來了哀泣的聲音。

「注意聽，是叮噹。」柯利說，「她因為溫蒂還活著，所以哭了呢。」

他們七嘴八舌地向彼得潘吐露叮噹的罪狀，彼得潘氣憤的模樣是他們前所未見的。

「叮噹貝爾，聽著，」彼得潘吼叫道，「我們不再是朋友了，我要妳永遠從我眼前消失。」

叮噹飛到了彼得潘的肩膀上苦苦哀求，但他將她揮開。一直到溫蒂又舉起手來，彼得潘才大發慈悲地說：「好吧，不必永遠，但至少要消失一個星期。」

妳以為叮噹貝爾會感激溫蒂嗎？噢，不，才不會呢，她反而更想使勁的擰她。

但是溫蒂現在這麼虛弱，該怎麼辦呢？

「我有個主意，」彼得潘說，「我們可以在她四周蓋一座小房子。」

其他男孩聽了都相當高興。有片刻的功夫，他們全都忙得像婚禮前一天的裁縫；他們東奔西跑，一下子到地底取棉被，一下到地面拾木柴，而在他們忙成一團時，約翰和麥可出現了。自從和其餘人分散後，他們兩人一直蹣跚地往前走，睡著，停了下來，驚醒，再往前走，再度睡著。

他們找到了彼得潘，自然就安心多了。

「哈囉，彼得潘。」他們向他打招呼。

「哈囉！」雖然彼得潘已把他們忘得差不多了，但還是很友善地回應。他正忙著用腳測量溫蒂有多高，好確定她需要多大的屋子。當然，他還會預留空間擺些桌子和椅子。約翰和麥可看著他。

「柯利，」彼得潘以最權威的聲音說，「帶這兩個男孩去幫忙蓋房子。」

「是的，老大。」

「蓋房子？」約翰不可思議地叫道。

「為了溫蒂。」柯利回答。

「為了溫蒂?」約翰愣住了。「天啊,她不過是個女孩子!」

柯利解釋:「這正是我們當她僕人的原因。」

「你們?當溫蒂的僕人?」

「對,」彼得潘說,「你們也是,跟他們去吧。」

這對驚詫的兄弟於是被拉去砍柴了。「先造椅子和爐圍,」彼得潘命令說,「這樣我們就能圍著它們蓋房子了。」

同時,樹林中到處都是砍柴的聲響,熱鬧非凡;蓋一間溫暖又舒適的小屋該具備的東西,幾乎全都擺在溫蒂腳邊了。

這間小屋相當漂亮,溫蒂待在裡面一定很舒適,雖然此刻他們已看不到她了。彼得潘來回地躂步巡視,命令男孩完成最後的工作。沒有一點能逃過他如老鷹般銳利的雙眼,除非整間小屋都完全妥當了。

「門上沒有門環。」彼得潘說。

男孩們都感到很慚愧,於是托托把他的鞋底取下來,便成了最適合的門把。現在完成了,他們想。

「每個人都要好好打扮，」彼得潘警告他們，「第一印象是非常重要的。」

彼得潘有禮地敲敲門；森林內一片寂靜，孩子們也都屏息無聲，只有在樹枝上偷看的叮噹貝爾公然發出輕蔑的嘲笑聲。

門打開了，一個女孩走了出來，是溫蒂。他們全都摘下帽子。

溫蒂露出驚訝的表情，這正是他們期望見到的。

「我在哪裡？」溫蒂說。

當然又是史萊特利首先答話。「溫蒂小姐，」他很快地回答，「我們為你蓋了這棟屋子。」

「這真是間可愛又迷人的小屋。」溫蒂說，這也正是他們期望聽到的。

「還有，我們都是妳的孩子。」雙胞胎嚷道。

隨後，所有人都跪了下來，舉起手懇求：「噢，溫蒂小姐，請當我們的母親。」

「我可以嗎？」溫蒂全身充滿母愛的光輝說道，「那當然是很有趣的，但是你們知道我不過是個小女孩啊，我沒有實際的經驗。」

「那不要緊。」彼得潘說，好像此時只有他一個人懂得這些事似的，其實他懂得最少。「我們需要的只是一個像母親般溫柔的人。」

「噢，親愛的。」溫蒂說，「你瞧，我覺得我正是不二人選了。」

「沒錯，沒錯。」所有人都嚷道，「我們早就看出來了。」

「很好，」溫蒂說，「我會盡力而為。你們這群頑皮的小鬼，馬上進來屋內吧；你們的腳一定都濕了。在你們上床前，我正好有時間把仙杜瑞拉的故事說完呢！」

第七章 地底之家

第二天，彼得潘做的第一件事，就是丈量溫蒂、約翰和麥可三人的身材，好找出適合他們的空心樹。當你找到適合的樹時，你只要在地面上吸口氣，就可以快速地滑下去，想要到上面來時，只要一吸一呼，身體就會蠕動上升。

但前提是你的體型與樹窟必須合適，所以彼得潘在測量體型就像在裁製衣服一般仔細：做衣服是要讓衣服合身，而現在是要讓樹合人，這便是唯一的不同。假如你找到適合的樹，千萬注意要保持著這個適合的狀態，溫蒂發現這點時相當高興，因為這讓全家人都保持著最佳的身材。

溫蒂和麥可第一次嘗試就找到合適的樹，但約翰則需要一些修改。

經過幾天的練習，他們都能夠像井裡的水桶一般地升降自如。他們漸漸愛上了地底之家，尤其是溫蒂。地底之家很大，有舒適的房間還有泥土地。男孩們把蘑菇拿來當椅子，用鋸掉的樹幹當作桌子。

廳裡有一個很大的壁爐，幾乎佔滿了整個房間的牆壁，你想從哪裡生火都可以，

溫蒂在火爐之間牽起了一條纖維揉製成的繩索，用來懸掛洗滌物。因為床幾乎要佔掉一半的空間，所以他們在白天就將床靠著牆立起來，到了傍晚六點半鐘才又放下來。

除了麥可，所有男孩都睡在這張床上，擠得就像魚罐頭裡的沙丁魚一般。翻身都有極嚴格的規則，由一個人發號施令，然後大家一起翻身。麥可本來也該睡在這張床上，但因為溫蒂想要一個小寶寶，而麥可年紀又最小，所以有段時間麥可都睡在搖籃裡。

牆上有一個比鳥籠大不了多少的凹洞，是叮噹貝爾的閨房。有一條小小的窗簾隔開了男孩的房間，讓挑剔的叮噹可以在換衣服時拉上。沒有一個女人，無論是多麼高大的女人，能再有這麼精緻的閨房了。

這一切對溫蒂來說都很有趣。這些吵鬧的男孩讓她有得忙呢，事實上，有好幾個禮拜，溫蒂除了夜晚帶隻襪子到地面上來，根本就沒出現在地面過。

溫蒂最喜歡的時刻，是在孩子們都上床後，獨自一人作些針線活兒。如她自己形容的，這時她才得以喘喘氣；她利用這段時間為孩子們做些新衣服，或者在褲子的膝蓋部位多縫上幾塊布，因為膝蓋部位都已經磨損不堪了。

溫蒂恐怕真的不是很牽掛她的父母：她相當有自信地認為，父母一定會永遠打開

一扇窗等待她回家，因此她很放心。有時她會感到不安，因為約翰對於父母的印象已變得很模糊，只把他們當成是從前認識的人似的，而麥可則全然忘記了，一直深信溫蒂就是自己的母親。為了解決這個問題，溫蒂設立了一個小學校，以他們的舊生活為主題，而不是拼寫或數學。

其他的男孩覺得這很好玩，堅持要加入，他們自備石板圍坐在桌旁，認真地思考並回答溫蒂寫在另一張石板上傳閱的問題。那些都是最基本的題目——「母親的眼睛曾經是什麼顏色？母親跟父親哪一個比較高？母親的頭髮是金黃色或深褐色？請盡量作答。」

彼得潘沒有參加考試。一方面是除了溫蒂以外，他討厭所有的母親，另一方面則是他是島上唯一不會拼音寫字的男孩，再簡單的字都不會，他對這種事一竅不通。

彼得潘經常獨自外出，回來時，你永遠無法斷定他是否剛結束一場冒險。偶爾，他會頭上紮著繃帶回家，溫蒂便會溫柔地跟他說話，用溫熱的水幫他清洗傷口，這時彼得潘會告訴她一段驚人的冒險故事。

我們提一下他們和印地安人在史萊特利峽谷所發生的故事好嗎？那是場流血的戰爭，特別的有趣，因為可以顯露出彼得潘的特殊之處，那就是，他會突然在戰爭中加

入對手的陣營。在峽谷時，當雙方勝負未分之時，彼得潘會突然叫道，「我今天是印地安人；托托，你呢？」托托回答，「我是印地安人；尼伯斯，你呢？」於是尼伯斯又說，「印地安人；雙胞胎，你們呢？」依此類推；最後他們全都變成印地安人了。

要不是真正的印地安人中了彼得潘的詭計，願意暫時充當一下迷路的男孩，這場戰役就結束了。他們再度開戰，戰火比之前更為猛烈。

又或者，我們可以談一下海盜為了毒殺孩子所烤的蛋糕，以及他們是如何一次又一次狡詐地把蛋糕放在顯眼的地方。但溫蒂總是會及時從孩子們的手中搶過蛋糕，所以蛋糕最後都失去了口感，變得跟石頭一樣硬，還可以拿來當飛彈發射，虎克船長就曾經在黑夜裡被擊中過。

我們該選擇哪一場冒險呢？最好的方式就是丟銅板決定吧。

我丟了銅板了，珊瑚湖冒險勝出。

第八章 美人魚的珊瑚湖

孩子們經常在美人魚的珊瑚湖上消磨夏季長日，多半的時間，他們都在游泳、漂浮或跟美人魚遊戲等等。不過你可別就此以為美人魚對這些孩子們很友善，其實正好相反。

觀賞人魚的最佳時刻是在月亮升起時，那時，人魚會發出奇特的哭泣聲；不過，此時的珊瑚湖對一般人來說相當危險。溫蒂知道這點，所以總會在天黑之前把孩子們帶離。

孩子們吃過午餐後，躺在岩石上休息片晌的畫面，看來也相當的美麗。溫蒂堅持他們吃過飯後要休息，就算吃飯只是假裝的，也要真的休息。於是他們便在陽光下臥著，身子閃閃發亮，溫蒂則神情威嚴地坐在一旁。

溫蒂正在縫紉時，珊瑚湖發生了騷動。水面顫了幾下，太陽消失了，陰影襲上湖面，水變冷了。溫蒂無法看清楚針孔了，她抬頭一看，向來充滿歡樂的珊瑚湖變得相

第八章 美人魚的珊瑚湖

當掙獰可怕。那不是夜晚的到來，情況似乎變得糟糕。

事實上，溫蒂應該立刻叫起孩子的，因爲危險正朝他們逼近，而且睡在寒冷的岩石上對孩子們的身體也不好。但溫蒂只是個年幼的母親，不懂得這點道理，她只覺得一定要嚴格遵守飯後休息半小時的規定。

幸好，這些男孩中有一個能在睡覺時用鼻子嗅出危險。彼得潘猶如狗般靈敏地清醒過來，他坐起身，然後發出警報聲，把所有人都叫醒。

「海盜！」彼得潘叫道。

「潛入水裡！」

轉眼間，只聽到幾條腿一閃，整個珊瑚湖很快地就沒了人影。溺囚岩好像遭人遺棄似地，孤孤單單地聳立在波濤洶湧的水裡。

船越來越靠近了，是海盜的小艇。船上有三個人，史密、史塔基和一個俘虜，老虎莉莉。老虎莉莉的手和腳都被綁住，她很清楚自己會有什麼下場。但是莉莉鎮定自若：她是酋長的女兒，死也要死得像個酋長的女兒，這就夠了。

海盜在她登上船時抓到她，她嘴裡還銜著一把刀。船上並沒有人守衛，因爲虎克船長吹噓說，他的名聲就足以讓所有東西退避三舍。現在，莉莉的例子更足以殺雞儆猴。到了晚上，另一聲哀嚎將讓虎克的名聲流傳得更遠。

這真是殘忍，竟然要把這麼漂亮的女孩丟到岩石上。莉莉的自尊心很強，絕不會求饒。

離岩石很近但是眼力所不能看到的地方，有兩顆頭正在水中忽現忽沒，是彼得潘和溫蒂。溫蒂頭一次見到這種悲劇，不禁哭了起來。彼得潘看過的悲劇可多了，只是他都忘光了。關於老虎莉莉的遭遇，他不像溫蒂那樣的感傷，他生氣的是，二個男生對付一個弱女子是不對的，所以他決定要救莉莉。

幾乎沒有彼得潘做不到的事情，他開始模仿虎克船長的聲音。

「放了她。」

「放了她？」

「是的，解開她的繩索，讓她走。」

「可是，船長──」

「立刻放了她，聽見沒有。」彼得潘嚷道，「否則我就用鐵鉤對付你。」

「是，是！」史密說著，就砍斷綁住老虎莉莉的細繩。老虎莉莉立刻如鰻魚一樣滑溜溜地繞過史塔基的腳，跳入水裡。

溫蒂看到彼得潘這麼聰明，心中很高興；但她知道彼得潘自己也很得意，還可能會忍不住歡呼幾聲而壞了好事，所以她立刻伸出手摀住他的嘴。她才伸出手，虎克的聲音就在珊瑚湖上響起「夥計們！」——這一回可不是彼得潘假扮的。

「夥計們！」叫聲又出現了一次。

溫蒂明白，真正的虎克船長來了。

虎克游到船旁，他的部下用照射燈指引他，他立刻爬上船。在燈籠的亮光中，溫蒂看見虎克船長的鐵鉤緊抓住船身；在虎克濕淋淋地從水中起身時，她看到了他邪惡黝黑的臉孔。溫蒂打著顫，很想要趕快離開，但彼得潘可不願逃跑。

彼得潘示意要溫蒂靜聽。

兩個海盜好奇地想知道，船長為什麼會過來找他們，但虎克卻用鐵鉤托著頭坐下來，顯得很沉悶的樣子。

「船長，怎麼了？」

最後，虎克終於惱怒地開口說話了。

「計劃失敗了，」他吼道，「那些男孩找來了一個母親。」

溫蒂雖然害怕，但仍滿心驕傲。

「噢，真是糟糕。」史塔基嚷道。

「什麼是母親？」無知的史密問。

就在這時，屬於夢幻鳥的巢正漂浮著，母鳥依然坐在裡頭。

「你看，」虎克回答史密，「那隻鳥就是母親。這是多好的一個教訓！鳥巢雖然掉落水裡，但是母鳥會遺棄鳥蛋跟巢離去嗎？答案是不會。」

史密大受感動，凝視著鳥巢與鳥兒自眼前漂流而過，但生性較多疑的史塔基則說：「假如那隻鳥是母親，牠在這附近打轉可能就是要幫助彼得潘。」

虎克有些畏縮。「沒錯，」他說，「那正是我害怕的。」

不過，史密接下來的提議又讓虎克重新振作。

「船長，」史密說，「難道我們不能把孩子的母親擄來做我們的母親嗎？」

「這個計劃好極了。」虎克叫了起來，聰明的腦袋裡立刻就定下了計策。「我們抓住小孩，把他們帶到船上，命令他們在舷上行走，溺死他們，這樣溫蒂就可以變成我們的母親了。」

「等等，那個印地安人在哪裡？」他突然問道。

虎克有時喜歡開玩笑，所以其他人以為他又在開玩笑了。

「船長，都弄好了，」史密諂媚地回答，「我們放走她啦。」

「放她走了?」虎克大叫。

「是你下令的。」水手膽怯地說。

「你在水中喊著要我們放她走啊!」史塔基說。

「可惡，」虎克暴跳如雷地說，「這裡發生什麼事了?」他的臉已經因為憤怒而漲紅，但他知道水手沒有說謊，所以不禁詫異起來。「夥計們，」他顫抖著說，「我並沒有下這樣的命令。」

「那真奇怪!」史密說，他們都驚慌失措。虎克特意提高音調，但聲音明顯地在發抖。

「今晚，出現在這座黑暗之湖上的鬼魂啊，」虎克叫道，「你聽到我的聲音了嗎?」

彼得潘應該要默不作聲的，但他當然不會這麼做，他立刻仿效虎克的聲音回答道，「我聽見了。」

「神秘的人物，你是誰呢?」虎克詢問。

「我是詹姆斯‧虎克，」有聲音回答道，「快樂羅傑號的船長。」

「你不是，你不是！」虎克粗聲粗氣地反駁。

「可惡的東西，」聲音喝斥道，「你再說一遍，我就把船錨插進你身子裡。」

虎克改採柔和的態度。「如果你是虎克，」他說話的語氣近乎謙卑，「那請告訴我，我又是誰呢？」

「一條鱈魚，」聲音又答，「你只是一條鱈魚。」

「一條鱈魚！」虎克駭然。他驕傲的靈魂就崩潰了，他看見部下正在遠離他。

「原來，我們擁戴的船長是一條鱈魚？」他們咕噥道，「這真是有損我們的自尊。」

虎克被自己養的狗反咬了一口，但是他雖然處在這麼悲慘的地位，他還是沒多加理會他們。對這樣可怕的指控，他需要的不是部下的信心，而是他對自己的信心，他覺得自己的自尊正一點一點的崩潰。「別丟下我。」他低聲向自己的自尊說道。

一如所有偉大的海盜，虎克凶殘的天性中帶著一絲女性氣質，這有時會帶給他一些直覺。他突然開始玩起猜謎遊戲。

「虎克，」他叫道，「你還有另一種聲音嗎？」

彼得潘永遠阻擋不了遊戲的誘惑，他快樂地以自己的聲音回答，「有啊。」

「那有另一個名字嗎？」

「有，有。」

「你是動物？蔬菜？還是礦物？」虎克問。

「都不是。」

「男人？」

「才不是。」這個回答帶著不屑。

「男孩？」

「沒錯。」

「普通的男孩？」

「才不！」

「特別的男孩？」

虎克已經完全搞糊塗了。

溫蒂感到相當苦惱，因為這回跑出來的答案是「答對了。」

「猜不到，猜不到！」彼得潘歡呼道，「你們放棄了嗎？」

「對，對，我們放棄了。」海盜們熱切地回答。

「好吧，那麼我告訴你們好了，」他叫道，「我是彼得潘。」

彼得潘！

一瞬間，虎克船長又重拾他的身分地位，史密跟史塔基又成了他忠實的部下。

「現在，我們一定要抓到彼得潘。」虎克咆哮，「史密，你下水去；史塔基，你看著船。無論生擒或死屍，都要把彼得潘給我帶來。」

虎克邊說邊跳腳，同時，又傳來彼得潘高興的聲音。

「男孩們，準備好了嗎？」

「好了，好了。」珊瑚湖各個角落傳來回應。

「那麼，開始攻擊。」

這場戰役很短，卻很慘烈。劍刃在水中與空中交錯互擊，兩個海盜與迷路的男孩們開戰，緊跟著聽到歡呼與吶喊聲。

彼得潘與虎克則有屬於他們的戰鬥。

奇怪的是，彼得潘與虎克在湖裡並沒有遇到對方。虎克爬到岩石上想喘一口氣，同時，彼得潘也爬上岩石另一端。

彼得潘並不害怕，這時候他只覺得愉快，他還高興得露出漂亮的貝齒呢。彼得潘抽出虎克腰際的刀，準備狠狠地刺擊時，突然發現自己站得比虎克還要高，他認為這樣的交戰並不公平，於是伸出手想拉虎克上來。

虎克趁機用鐵鉤抓傷他。

彼得潘愣住了，不是因為手上的傷，而是虎克這種行為太下流卑鄙了。他茫然地站著，慌亂地睜大眼。每個孩子第一次遇到這種不公平待遇時，都會有這種反應。

虎克的鐵鉤趁機又攻擊他。如果不是滴答聲，彼得潘就被虎克殺死了。

幾分鐘之後，其他的男孩就看到虎克拚命的向船邊游去。他凶惡的臉上少了得意的神情，只是蒼白的恐怖，因為一隻鱷魚正緊追著他。

平常，男孩會跟在旁邊看好戲，但現在他們卻感到不安，因為彼得潘和溫蒂不見了，他們只能沿著珊瑚湖，大聲喊著他們兩人的名字尋覓。他們找到了海盜的小艇，於是坐船返家，沿途不斷喊著「彼得潘、溫蒂」，但是除了美人魚嘲弄的笑聲外，並沒有得到任何回應。「他們可能游回去或飛回去了。」男孩下了結論。他們並不緊張，彼得潘總是讓人可以信賴。

他們的聲音遠去後，珊瑚湖又恢復了一片死寂，隨後傳來一陣微弱的叫聲。

「救命，救命！」

兩個小小的人體正向岩石上衝撞；女孩已暈厥，臥在男孩的臂上。彼得潘用盡最後一絲力氣將溫蒂拉上岩石後，便在她身旁躺了下來。他曉得他們很快就會被淹死，但卻無能為力。

他們肩並肩地躺在一塊起，一隻美人魚抓住溫蒂的腳，緩緩地將她拉入水中。彼得潘察覺到溫蒂從身旁溜下去了，猛然醒了過來，及時地將她拉回來。

「溫蒂，我們現在是在溺囚岩上，」他說，「但是水位越來越高，不久這塊岩石就會被淹沒了。」

「那我們得趕快離開。」她幾乎是開心地回答。

「沒錯。」彼得潘虛弱地答道。

「彼得潘，我們要用飛的還是游的呢？」

他只好告訴她實話。「溫蒂，妳覺得若沒有我的幫助，妳可以游泳或飛到島上嗎？」

溫蒂只得承認，自己實在太疲倦了。

彼得潘呻吟了一下。

「怎麼了？」溫蒂問，立刻擔心起彼得潘。

「溫蒂，我幫不了妳。虎克害我受傷了，我游不動，飛不了。」

「你是說我們兩個會一塊兒淹死嗎?」

他們用手搗住眼睛，不敢看那恐怖的景象，以為不久就要同歸於盡。他們就這樣坐著，忽然有個東西像吻一般輕柔地拂拭了彼得潘，而且還停在那裡，好像在輕聲說著，「我幫得上忙嗎?」

那是一只風箏的尾巴，這風箏是麥可幾天前做的。它後來掙脫了麥可的手，隨著風飄走了。

「是麥可的風箏。」

「這個風箏可以將麥可從地面拉起來，」彼得潘提不起勁兒的說，忽然他就抓住風箏的尾巴，將它拉過來。

「那它一定可以拉得動妳!」

「是我們!」

「它一次拉不動兩個人，麥可跟柯利試過了。」

「那我們抽籤吧。」溫蒂勇敢地說。

「不行，你是女人。」彼得潘已經把風箏尾巴繫在溫蒂身上。溫蒂靠向他，不想獨自離開；但是彼得潘說了聲「再見，溫蒂。」就推了她一把，幾分鐘的功夫，溫蒂便飄走不見了。彼得潘獨自一人留在岩石上。

岩石露出水面的範圍越來越小了，很快就會淹沒。彼得潘雖然跟其他的男孩很不一樣，但他終究還是會害怕。不過，很快地，興奮取代了害怕。他就矗立在岩石上，臉上露出笑容，心裡的小鼓敲動著說：「死亡是最偉大的冒險。」

第九章 夢幻鳥

彼得潘最後聽到的聲音，是美人魚逐一回到海底寢室休息的聲響。水位漸漸升高，淹到他的腳跟了。在被淹之前，彼得潘爲了打發時間，開始觀察湖面上漂流的一件東西。彼得潘覺得，那是一張漂流的紙片，也許是風箏的一部份，他無聊地估計起它漂到岸邊所需的時間。

其實，那並不是一張紙，而是夢幻鳥，牠正拚命地將鳥巢划向彼得潘。自從鳥巢掉落水裡後，牠就學會鼓動翅膀來划行，竟然也可勉強地前進。等到彼得潘認出牠時，牠已筋疲力盡了。夢幻鳥是趕來解救彼得潘的，牠打算把鳥巢讓給他，雖然裡面還有鳥蛋。

夢幻鳥靠近時，開始叫起彼得潘的名字，彼得潘也回應牠。當然，他們都不懂對方的語言。

第九章　夢幻鳥

「我要你——進鳥巢——來，」夢幻鳥盡可能地叫得又慢又清楚，「你就能——漂到——岸上去——。」

「你在吱吱叫什麼？」彼得潘回答。

「我——要——你——」夢幻鳥又將話重複了一次。

於是，彼得潘也試著慢慢將話說清楚。「你——說——什——麼？」

夢幻鳥發脾氣了，牠們的脾氣向來就不好。「你這個愚蠢的笨蛋，」牠尖叫起來，「你為什麼不照著我的話做？」

彼得潘感覺到夢幻鳥正在罵他，於是生氣地反駁：「你也是！」

然後，他們不約而同地罵出同樣的話。「你閉嘴！」

儘管如此，夢幻鳥還是決心要幫彼得潘的忙，於是牠用盡最後一絲力氣將鳥巢划至岩石邊。牠飛上天空，把鳥蛋留在鳥巢中，清楚地表達出自己的意思。

彼得潘終於懂了，他抓住鳥巢，向飛在前方的夢幻鳥揮手感謝。

鳥巢裡面有兩顆大白蛋，彼得潘舉起它們，在心裡盤算該怎麼做。夢幻鳥用翅膀遮住臉，怕看到自己的蛋消失，但牠還是忍不住從羽毛的縫隙向下窺探。

在彼得潘旁邊的岩石上，有一頂寬邊的防水帽，這是史塔基留下的。彼得潘將鳥蛋放進這頂帽子裡，再將帽子放到水上，任它優雅地漂流。

夢幻鳥看出彼得潘的用意，牠尖叫著表達自己的感激；彼得潘也以歡呼回應牠。接著他就爬進鳥巢裡。此時，夢幻鳥也飛向那頂帽子，再次安穩地落坐到鳥蛋上。他們皆大歡喜地朝不同方向離開。

彼得潘一上岸，就把鳥巢停在夢幻鳥能輕易找到的地方；不過，那頂防水帽實在太舒服了，夢幻鳥已捨棄了原先的鳥巢，任它四處漂流，直到粉碎。

彼得潘回到地底之家的時候，溫蒂也差不多剛好被風箏東飄西飄地帶回，他們獲得了其他人熱烈的歡迎。每個男孩都急欲吐露自己的冒險故事，不過最了不起的事蹟就是他們已晚睡了好個小時，這使他們高興極了，所以他們又施了一些詭計，比如說到處找繃帶，好多拖延一點時間再上床。溫蒂雖然很高興看到他們都平安無事地回家，但她仍舊不喜歡他們熬夜。她急得直叫：「去睡覺，去睡覺。」語氣不容違逆。

珊瑚湖事件發生後的一個重要結果，就是他們跟印地安人成了朋友。彼得潘救了老虎莉莉一命，所以她跟她的勇士願意為他效勞。海盜顯然會在最近就展開反擊，印地安人徹夜坐在地面上守衛地底之家，防止海盜襲擊。

第十章　溫蒂的故事

「你們注意聽唷！」溫蒂開始講故事，她的腳邊坐著麥可，其他七個男孩則躺在床上，「從前從前，有一位紳士——」

「我希望那是一個淑女。」柯利說。

「安靜，」溫蒂斥責道，又繼續說，「還有一位淑女，然後——」

「噢，媽咪。」雙胞胎之一叫起來，「妳是說另外還有一位淑女，是嗎？她沒死，對吧？」

「安靜點吧。」彼得潘斥責道，不管那個故事在他眼中有多麼噁心，他仍想讓溫蒂順利地說故事。

「他們結婚了，」溫蒂解釋說，「你們想他們會生下什麼？」

「白老鼠。」尼伯斯靈機一動回答。

「不是。」

「真是難猜。」托托心裡早就背熟這個故事了，但他仍如此說。

「安靜，托托。達林夫婦擁有三個子嗣。」

「什麼是子嗣？」

「你們就是一個例子啊，雙胞胎。」

「噢，天哪，」溫蒂嘆了口氣說，「這三個小孩有一個忠誠的保母，叫娜娜。達林先生為了某件小事對娜娜發脾氣，還把牠綁在院子裡，所以三個小孩都飛走了。」

「這故事真是帥呆了。」尼伯斯說。

「他們飛走後，」溫蒂繼續說道，「來到了夢幻島，這是迷路的小孩生活的地方。」

「我知道了。」

「我只知道他們來了，」柯利興奮地迸出話來，「但不知道他們怎麼來的，現在我知道了。」

「喔，溫蒂，」托托叫道，「其中一個迷路的小孩是叫托托嗎？」

「是的，沒錯。」

「我也在故事裡了，哈哈，我在故事裡了，尼伯斯。」

「安靜。現在，我要你們想想，那對不幸的父母在看到孩子都飛走後，會有什麼感受。」

「唉！」儘管他們沒有真的想到那對不快樂的父母，但還是都發出了哀嘆。

「我覺得結局一定很悲傷。」另一個雙胞胎說道。

「如果你們知道母愛有多偉大，」溫蒂得意地告訴他們，「你們就一無所懼了。」她現在提到了彼得潘最討厭的部分。

「我們的女主角知道，」溫蒂自負地說道，「母親總會為孩子留一扇窗，等待他們回家，所以他們可以安心地在夢幻島待上好幾年，享受快樂的時光。」

「那三個孩子曾經回去過嗎？」

「現在，」溫蒂輕輕地抱住自己的胳膊說，「就讓我們來猜一猜未來的發展吧。」所有的孩子都抖擻起精神，想猜猜看未來。於是，溫蒂手指著上方說道，

「『親愛的弟弟，育兒室那扇窗戶還開著呢。啊，我們之前對母愛有著至高無上的信任，現在是回報的時候了。』所以他們就飛回父母身旁，快樂的結局是筆墨無法形容的，故事就到此結束吧。」

「彼得潘，怎麼啦？」溫蒂以為彼得潘不舒服，緊張地叫了起來。

角落傳來彼得潘低沉的呻吟聲。

「不是那種不舒服。」彼得潘慘然答道。

「要不然呢？」

「溫蒂，妳對母親的見解是錯的。」

彼得潘這句話相當驚人，所有人都驚恐地圍到他身邊。於是，彼得潘直率地說出迄今尚未吐露過的秘密。

「在很久以前，」彼得潘說，「我也跟你們一樣認為母親總是會留一扇窗等我回去，所以我在外流連忘返，很久之後才回家。結果窗戶已經上了鎖，我的母親早忘記我了，睡在我床上的是另一個小男孩。」

「你確定母親是這樣的嗎？」

「嗯。」

這就是母親的真面目。真是壞蛋！

所以，最好還是小心為妙，沒有人比小孩子更清楚何時該讓步的。「溫蒂，我們回家吧。」

「好的。」約翰和麥可齊聲叫道。

「不會是今晚吧？」溫蒂摟著他們回答。

迷路的小孩子惶恐地問。他們心裡都明白，沒有母親他們也可以過得很好，只有母親才會以為，小孩子沒有她們就活不下去。

「立刻就走，」溫蒂堅決地回答，因為她的腦中已浮現了可怕的念頭：「或許母親現在已經難過得不成人形了。」

恐懼使得她忘記了彼得潘的感受，她很無情地對彼得潘說：「彼得潘，你可以幫我們做準備嗎？」

「如果妳希望的話。」彼得潘冷回，那態度就好像她要他傳遞堅果時一般。

他們兩人之間連一句告別話都沒有！如果溫蒂不介意分離，彼得潘也要做給她看，假裝他也不在乎。

「溫蒂，」彼得潘來回地踱步，「我已經請印地安人帶你們走過樹林，這樣你們就不會因為長途飛行而累壞。」

「謝謝你，彼得潘。」

「然後，」他以一種不容違背的嚴厲聲調繼續扼要地說，「叮噹貝爾會領你們過海。尼伯斯，把叮噹叫起來。」

同時，男孩們都無助地看著溫蒂，她正在幫麥可和約翰打點。他們感到悲傷。

「各位，」溫蒂說，「如果你們願意跟我一起走，我應該有把握讓我的父母收養你們。」

這句話是特別說給彼得潘聽的，但其他的孩子都沒想到他，馬上高興地跳起來。

「彼得潘，我們可以走嗎？」男孩們乞求地問彼得潘。

「可以啊。」彼得潘帶著痛苦的微笑說。於是，所有的孩子都立刻去打點東西。

「現在，彼得潘，」溫蒂說，心想什麼都已經整理好了，「在你動身之前，我要給你喝藥。」溫蒂很喜歡給他們喝藥，而且總是給過量。事實上，那些藥只不過是裝在葫蘆瓶裡的清水罷了。溫蒂總是要搖搖葫蘆瓶，算算流了幾滴水出來，以確保療效。然而，這一回溫蒂卻沒有給彼得潘喝藥，因為當她正在準備藥時，卻看到彼得潘臉上的神情，她的心不禁爲之下沉。

「彼得潘，去收拾行李。」她顫抖著身子說。

「不，」彼得潘裝得很冷漠，「溫蒂，我不會跟妳一起走。」

接著，大家都知道這個消息了。

「彼得潘不一起走。」

彼得潘不走！ 其他男孩背後挑著一根綁了包袱的棒子，茫然地站著看彼得潘，心中想到的第一個念頭是，若是彼得潘不走，他可能會改變心意，也不讓他們離開。

「現在，別吵別哭，」彼得潘說，「再見了，溫蒂。」

他們的對話就只有這樣，隨後就是一陣令人難受的沉默。然而，彼得潘不是會在人前悲慟的人。「叮噹貝爾，妳準備好了嗎？」他叫道。

「好啦，好啦。」

「那就帶路吧。」

叮噹飛上了最近的一棵樹，但卻沒有人跟隨她動作，因為海盜正對印地安人展開猛烈的攻擊。本來還一片寧靜的地面，現在已充滿了刀兵相接的聲響。地底下一片死寂。每個人都張大了嘴，愣住了。

第十一章 孩子被捉走了

海盜的攻擊讓人措手不及，但是也證明了無恥的虎克指揮不當，因為，想要出其不意地襲擊印地安人是只憑白人的智慧根本做不到的事情。

在漫漫的長夜裡，印地安人的偵查兵開始像蛇一樣蜿蜒前進，一聲不響地穿過草叢，甚至無須砍斷一根雜草。他們走過的灌木叢在他們身後合攏，安靜地猶如沙子掉進鼴鼠洞一般。萬籟俱寂，除了偶爾可以聽到偵查兵維妙維肖地模仿狼嚎外，就再也聽不到別的聲音了。

獵人頭族們對虎克的名聲深信不疑，所以他們當晚的行動正好跟虎克的行動成了強烈的對比，他們部落該做的事情都完成了：一聽見海盜踩上枯樹枝的聲音，印地安人就立刻知道海盜來到島上了。霎時，他們開始發出狼叫，聯絡同伴。偵查兵穿上軟靴，悄悄地偵查過虎克登陸的地點以及其與地底之家之間的路段，發現其中只有一個小山丘有溪流經過，所以虎克別無選擇，一定會在這裡駐紮，等待黎明。

於是，印地安人巧妙地部署妥當後，主要的人馬就裹著毯子，充滿氣概地坐在地底之家上方，等待廝殺的時刻來臨。多數的印地安人依然清醒，但是有些人已經墜入夢鄉，作著如何在天破曉之際嚴刑拷打虎克的春秋大夢，但是卻冷不防地被狡詐的虎克捷足先登了。從後來那些逃過大屠殺的偵查兵口中得知，虎克在昏黑的光線下應該有看到那個河水穿越的山丘，但是他卻沒有在那裡駐紮休息。在虎克狡猾的心裡，自始至終就沒想過要等到印地安人先攻擊，他甚至無法等到天亮再開戰，他的策略是立刻開戰。

在老虎莉莉的身邊圍著數十個勇敢的戰士，他們猛然驚見到奸詐的海盜直撲而來。他們立即睜大了眼，不再幻想著迷濛的勝利，要嚴刑拷打虎克是不可能的了。

此刻，是他們打獵的好機會——他們知道這一點；但身為印地安人，他們絕不輕舉妄動。他們若快點排成隊形，就很難讓敵人攻破，但是部落的傳統使他們不肯這麼做。

族史上規定，高貴的印地安人在白種人出現時，不可以表現出驚慌的樣子。他們勇敢地守住傳統，然後才舉起武器，發出的戰嚎撕裂了寧靜的空氣，但是一切都太遲了。

這個夜晚尚未結束，因為虎克船長的目標並不是印地安人；那些印地安人只不過是一些蜜蜂，他的目標可是蜂蜜呢！他要的是彼得潘、溫蒂及那群孩子，但最主要的

第十一章 孩子被捉走了

還是彼得潘。

彼得潘只不過是個小孩子，這不禁讓人猜測起虎克為何如此憎恨他的原因。的確，彼得潘是害虎克船長的手臂被鱷魚吃掉了，但是就算虎克因此少了一隻手臂，或著因為鱷魚的糾纏不休而多了一份不安全感，但是依然無法解釋他為何會對彼得潘如此的憎恨。答案是，彼得潘一定有什麼讓虎克特別發怒的地方——絕對不是彼得潘的勇氣，也不是他迷人的外表，更不是……，無須多加揣測，我們都知道答案是什麼，那就是彼得潘的傲氣。

虎克最恨這一點，氣到連鐵鉤都在顫抖，在夜晚時更會像隻蟲子般攪亂他的心房。只要彼得潘還活著，虎克就覺得自己像隻牢籠裡的困獅，眼睜睜地看著麻雀飛進來搗亂。

現在，問題來了，他或他的部下要怎麼鑽進樹洞裡面呢？虎克船長以兇狠的目光環視著部下，想要找出最瘦的一個。部下全都侷促不安地扭動身子，他們知道虎克絕對會毫不遲疑地將他們硬塞到樹洞裡去。

這時候，那些小男孩又在做什麼呢？戰爭剛開始的時候，我們就已經看到他們全都張著嘴楞住了，而且還伸著手臂祈求彼得潘別走；現在，他們的嘴巴已經闔上，胳膊也垂下來了。

到底是哪一邊贏了呢？

海盜們在樹洞旁熱切地偷聽，聽到了男孩們發出的問題，而，天啊，他們也聽到了彼得潘的回答。

「如果是印地安人贏了，」彼得潘說，「他們會打鼓來宣示勝利。」

史密早就找到了鼓，正坐在上面哩。「你再也聽不到鼓聲了。」他低語，當然，他的聲音小的讓人聽不見，因為虎克要他們保持安靜。但沒想到虎克卻指示史密敲鼓。史密後來才領悟這個命令有多麼狡詐，這個頭腦簡單的人從未如此尊敬虎克過。

史密敲了兩次鼓，接著就停了下來，高興地聆聽地底下的動靜。

「鼓聲，」海盜聽到彼得潘叫道，「印地安人贏了。」

孩子們興奮的歡呼，聲音聽在地面上的海盜耳中簡直就像是天籟，隨後，孩子開始跟彼得潘道別。海盜聽了有點困惑，但隨即就被喜悅掩蓋過去，因為敵人要出來了。他們露出得意的笑容，開始摩拳擦掌。虎克很快地輕聲下了命令：一個人守一株樹，其餘的人以間距兩碼的距離排成一線。

第十二章 你相信仙子嗎？

第一個從樹裡冒出頭的是柯利，他一出來就落入西柯的手裡，然後被丟到史密手上，跟著又到了史塔基手中，接下來又被丟到比爾喬克的手中，然後又落到努都的手裡，就這樣被丟來丟去，直到最後，才被扔到一個黑人海盜的腳邊。每個從樹中出現的男孩都遇到相同的命運，同時有好幾個男孩被扔到空中，好像工人在傳貨一樣。

溫蒂最後才出現，她得到的待遇很不同。虎克已假惺惺的禮拜，朝溫蒂摘下帽子，並伸出手臂攙著她走到其他人被囚禁的地方。他故意擺出高貴的樣子，讓溫蒂著迷得幾乎忘了尖叫。畢竟，她只不過是個小女孩。

如果她那時驕傲地甩開虎克的手，她可能就會跟其他孩子一樣被拋至空中，由水手一個接一個傳到黑人海盜腳邊，那麼虎克也不會出現在被綑綁起來的孩子面前了；如果虎克沒有出現在這些孩子們面前，他就不會發現史萊特利的秘密；假如沒有發現那個秘密，他就無法對付彼得潘了。

海盜為了防止孩子飛走，要他們拱起著身子，再將他們牢牢綁住。為了綁住他們，黑人海盜將一條繩索平均分成九段。綁人的動作進行得很順利，但輪到史萊特利時，問題就出現了。黑人海盜此時已汗流浹背，因為他在綑綁史萊特利時，剛想用力把這部分綑緊，另一部分就突了出來，不過，虎克的雙唇卻因為勝利而邪惡地笑了。

虎克看著史萊特利，心緒活動起來，他歡喜的模樣顯示出，他已經看穿史萊特利的秘密。史萊特利知道虎克已經發現，像他這麼胖的男孩可以使用的樹，一般人一定也可以來去自如。

發現了這一點，虎克告訴自己，彼得潘終究會落在他的手裡。不過，他並沒有將心裡的邪惡計劃說說出口。他只是示意要部下帶俘虜回到船上，他好獨自行事。

孩子們就被扔到小屋裡頭，由四個強壯的海盜扛著走，其他人跟在後頭。海盜一邊合唱惹人厭的音調，一邊穿過樹林離去。

現在，虎克獨自一人時，他所做的第一件事就是躡腳走到史萊特利的樹旁，想試試自己可不可以鑽進去。他沉思了好久，還把帽子摘下來放在草地上，讓微風拂過他的頭髮，讓他清醒一下。彼得潘睡著了嗎？還是正拿著刀等在史萊特利的樹下？

除非親自到地下去，否則沒有辦法得知答案。虎克輕輕地將外套扔到地上，咬緊

嘴唇，幾乎都要咬出血來，然後鑽進樹洞裡。

他平平安安地滑到樹幹旁，站穩腳步，順了順差點停止的呼吸。他的雙眼逐漸適應了屋內微弱的燈光，這才逐漸看清楚屋裡的一切；不過，虎克的目光只停在一樣東西上面——他找了好久才看到的——一張大床。床上躺著熟睡的彼得潘。

彼得潘對地面上的慘劇一無所知，其他人離開後，他還高興地吹了一會兒笛子，無疑地，他只是在徒勞無功地證明自己並不在乎。後來，他決定不吃藥了，這樣才能報復溫蒂。彼得潘幾乎要哭出來，但一想到如果他笑了，溫蒂會多麼生氣，他就故意開始大笑，笑到一半就在床上睡著了。

偶爾——雖然不是常有的事——彼得潘也會作夢，夢境比其他男孩的夢更為悲傷。他會連續好幾個小時無法脫離這些夢境，一直不停地痛哭。這時候，溫蒂會將他抱下床，讓他趴在大腿上，溫柔地安慰他。不過這一回，彼得潘完全沒有作夢。他的一隻胳臂落到床沿下，一隻腳拱了起來，張開的嘴角浮上一抹未完的笑意，露出裡面的小貝齒。

因此，虎克發現彼得潘時，他正處於毫無防備的狀態。虎克安靜地站在樹幹旁，望著屋子另一方的敵人。彼得潘睡覺的模樣，實在太令虎克討厭了。彼得潘嘴巴張得開開的，手臂垂落，膝蓋拱了起來——對一個敏感的人來說，這些動作合起來看實在是驕傲無禮，顯然是一種冒犯。

儘管床前有一盞燈發出微弱的光芒，虎克四周仍然一片黑暗。他悄悄地踏出第一步時，就發現遇到了障礙——史萊特利的樹幹上有一扇門。那扇門並沒有完全擋住洞口，所以剛才虎克是透過門縫朝屋內看，也就忽略了這扇門。他又憤怒地發現，門的門閂很低，他構不著，他氣壞了。

咦，那是什麼？虎克灼熱的目光立刻注意到，附近的架子上放著彼得潘的藥。他立即明白那是什麼東西，也很快就知道，彼得潘已完全落入自己手裡。

虎克在彼得潘的茶杯裡滴了五滴藥，手因為興奮而不停顫抖。他滴藥時避免去看熟睡中的彼得潘，倒不是怕同情心使自己下不了手，而是害怕毒藥灑了出來。隨後，他幸災樂禍地瞪了彼得潘好長一段時間，才轉過身，困難地蠕動身子爬上樹。當他回到地面時，還真像從洞裡跑出了一個魔鬼。

彼得潘仍繼續沉睡。燈光忽明忽滅，最後完全熄滅，使得整個室內伸手不見五指，但彼得潘仍繼續熟睡。一直到鱷魚肚子裡的鐘響了十點後，他才猛然在床上坐起身，莫名其妙清醒過來。他的樹幹門上傳來一陣謹慎小聲的敲門聲。

儘管敲門聲聽來謹慎輕柔，但在靜寂的深夜中，還是有點兒可怕。彼得潘四處摸索匕首，等到握住刀子之後，他才開口。「是誰？」

「彼得潘，讓我進去。」

是叮噹，彼得潘很快地開了門。叮噹緊張地溜進來，臉色泛紅，衣服上沾滿了泥巴。

「發生什麼事了？」

「噢，你絕對想不到。」叮噹尖叫，並給彼得潘三次猜答案的機會。「快說！」

彼得潘大吼；於是，叮噹用一句不合文法的長句——猶如魔術師從嘴巴裡拉出的緞帶一樣長——說出溫蒂及其他男孩被捉走的事。

「我去救她。」彼得潘嚷道，跳起來拿他的武器。同時，他想到他能做一些取悅溫蒂的事情——他可以先把藥喝光。

他的手握住那致命的藥杯。

「不要！」叮噹貝爾大叫，她已經聽到虎克在走出樹林時，一邊自言自語的話。

「為什麼？」

「有毒。」

「有毒？誰能下毒？」

「虎克。」

「別傻了，虎克怎麼能到這裡來？」

天哪，這一點叮噹貝爾也無法解釋，連她也不知道史萊特利的秘密。儘管如此，

虎克的話無須懷疑，藥裡一定有毒。

「況且，」彼得潘很有自信地說，「我根本就沒真正睡著呀。」

彼得潘舉起茶杯。沒時間多說了，先行動再說。叮噹一步搶上前，擋在彼得潘的

嘴唇與杯子之間，一口氣把藥喝光光。

「天啊，叮噹，妳怎麼可以喝我的藥？」

不過，叮噹沒有回答，她已經在空中暈倒了。

「妳怎麼了？」彼得潘恐懼地大叫。

「彼得潘，藥被下毒了，」叮噹輕聲答道，「現在我快死了。」

「噢，叮噹，妳是為了救我？」

「是的。」

「叮噹，為什麼？」

叮噹的翅膀已經撐不住自己的重量，但為了回答彼得潘的問題，她勉強飛到彼得潘肩上，憐愛地咬了他下巴一口。隨後，她就蹣跚地回到自己的寢室，躺在床上。

她在他耳邊低語說，「你這個傻瓜。」

彼得潘難過地蹲在叮噹身旁，整個頭幾乎佔滿了叮噹的房間。叮噹身上的光芒逐漸黯淡，他知道，光芒一消失，叮噹就死了。叮噹很高興看到彼得潘為她流淚，她伸出纖細的手指，讓淚珠流過自己的手。

叮噹的聲音變得十分低沉，一開始彼得潘還聽不清楚她說什麼。接著，他就聽懂了。

叮噹說，如果孩子們還相信仙子的存在，那她就能再度好起來。

彼得潘伸出雙臂。周遭並沒有孩子，現在又是半夜，不過，他召喚了所有夢見夢幻島的孩子，以及穿上睡衣的男孩女孩，還有掛在樹上育嬰袋裡的印地安寶寶。

「你們相信仙子的存在嗎？」彼得潘問。

叮噹猛然從床上坐起身，等待命運的判決。她在腦中幻想著正面的答案，但下一秒又開始擔憂。

「你覺得呢？」她問彼得潘。

「如果你們相信，」彼得潘對孩子大喊，「就拍拍手，不要讓叮噹死掉。」

許多人拍手。有些人沒有。

拍手聲乍然終止，似乎有許多母親緊張地衝入育兒室，查看到底發生了什麼事情，不過，叮噹已經獲救了。她的聲音先是越來越清晰有力，隨後，她跳下床，比以往更加快樂、有活力地在房裡飛舞。她並沒有想到要謝謝那些相信仙子的小孩，只想到要去找那些對仙子表示不屑的人算帳。

「現在，我們去救溫蒂吧。」

天空中雲層密佈，月亮在其間移走。彼得潘全副武裝地爬上地面，身上只穿著少少的衣物，準備開始冒險之旅。如果可以選擇，他不會選在這個夜晚冒險。他原想在離地面不遠處飛行，這樣眼下的事物就可以一目了然；但在月光忽隱忽現的情況下，低飛意味著他的影子會映在樹林裡，打擾到那些小鳥，引起敵人的注意。

他沒有別的辦法，只好模仿印地安人向前爬，他在這方面可是個行家。鱷魚從彼得潘身旁經過，除此之外，周遭沒有任何生物，甚至沒有任何聲音，任何動靜。彼得潘明白，死亡就在前方等著他，也或許會從背後跟上來。

彼得潘發誓道，「這次，我一定要跟虎克一決生死。」

第十三章 海盜船

一盞燈籠的綠光斜射在海盜河口的吉德灣上，映射出泊在淺水處的快樂羅傑號。

黑夜包圍了船隻，岸邊聽不到船上任何一點聲音。其實，船上除了縫紉機嘎嘎轉動的聲音外，虎克也不准有屬下發出聲音。史密正坐在縫紉機旁勤奮地工作，整個畫面看來就像是一幅居家畫面。

虎克在甲板上散步沉思。噢，他是個深不可測的男人。這是屬於他的勝利時刻：彼得潘已經從他眼前消失了，其他的男孩都在船上等著受死。從他馴服巴貝鳩以後，這一回可算是他最驚人的戰績了。

虎克經常會在寂靜的夜裡，在甲板上一邊散步一邊跟自己對談。這都是因為他太孤單了。他的部下包圍著他時，這個難以理解的男人會益發覺得寂寞——那些部下的社會地位比他差多了。

虎克其實不是他的真實姓名。即使是在現在，若他的真實身分曝光，也可能會轟動全國。虎克曾進過一所知名的公立學校，學校的一些傳統仍如衣服一般附在他的身上，他也的確最重視衣著。因此，就算是現在，若他攻入一艘船時所穿的衣服與征服它時相同，他認為這就是一種冒犯。此外，他散步時也會保持高貴的姿態。但最重要的是，他仍保有良好的禮儀。

禮儀！無論虎克有多麼墮落，他仍然知道，禮儀是最重要的。

他內心深處，好像聽到了生鏽的船門發出嘎嘎聲響，然後，門後傳來一陣冷酷的拍——拍——拍聲，就像失眠的人腦中出現的錘擊聲。「你今天有保持禮貌嗎？」他們永遠都會先這麼問道。

最令人不安的是，只顧著追求禮貌，不也算是一種失禮嗎？

他一直受這個問題所苦，這個在他體內的爪子比手上的鐵鉤還要銳利。當它開始折磨他的內心時，他油膩的臉上就會留下汗水，沾到了緊身衣。他通常會用袖子揩揩臉，但卻無法控制自己的眼淚。

他腦中浮現自己會早死的預感，好像彼得潘的賭咒已經傳到了船上。虎克忽然有一個絕望的念頭，想發表一篇遺言，以免死到臨頭沒有時間寫。

「沒有一個小孩子愛我。」

奇怪的是，他竟然會想到這一點，以前他從不會為這一點苦惱的；也許是縫紉機的聲音害得他胡思亂想。他一邊瞪著安靜縫衣裳的史密，一邊自言自語了好久，深信所有的小孩子都怕他。

怕他！怕史密！那個夜晚被捉到船上的孩子都喜歡上了史密。史密用言語嚇他們，用手心打他們，但孩子卻更黏著他，麥可還試過要搶他的眼鏡哩。

告訴可憐的史密，孩子們覺得他很可愛吧！虎克很想這麼做，但又覺得這句話對一個海盜有點兒殘忍。相反地，他試圖在心頭解開這個謎題：為什麼孩子們會覺得史密很可愛呢？一個可怕的答案忽然自動跑出來：「禮貌？」

難道說這個水手有著良好的禮儀卻不自知嗎？

虎克憤怒地叫了一聲，舉起鐵爪朝史密頭上撲過去，但他沒有繼續動作，阻止他的是心底的聲音：「只因為一個人有禮儀而去傷害他，這算什麼呢？」

「無禮！」

悶悶不樂的虎克一陣虛脫無力，覺得自己就像落花一般癱了。

他的部下以為他洩氣了，就鬆了紀律，開始喝酒狂歡，這使得虎克立刻恢復清醒，好像有一桶冷水自他身上澆下來，把他所有弱點都沖掉了。

「安靜一點，你們這討人厭的傢伙。」虎克叫道，「要不然我就拿鐵爪對付你們。」絮聒不休的聲音立刻靜了下來。「有沒有把小孩都關起來，以免他們飛走？」

「有的，有的。」

「現在把他們拖出來。」

除了溫蒂以外，一群可憐的俘虜都被海盜從囚禁室拖出，在虎克面前排成一列。

「那麼，你們這幾個小子，」虎克乾脆地說，「你們今晚有六個人要準備矇眼走舷板，不過呢，我有多餘的空缺可以僱用兩個男孩。你們誰想留下？」

「不要沒必要地惹怒他。」溫蒂在囚禁室中一直這樣告誡孩子們，所以托托就很有禮貌地往前踏了一步回應虎克。只是，他一點兒都不想當這個男人的屬下，忽然，他靈機一動，知道得把責任推到不在場的人身上。

因此，托托很慎重地解釋道：「先生，你知道，我想我的母親一定不願我當海盜。史萊特利，你的母親願意讓你當海盜嗎？」

他向史萊特利眨眨眼，史萊特利哀傷地回答：「我想她不會願意的。」一副他也很希望不是這樣似的。

「少說廢話！」虎克咆哮道，其他人只好住嘴。「就是你了，」虎克指著約翰說，「你看起來好像還有點勇氣。親愛的小朋友，你從沒想過當個海盜嗎？」

其實，約翰有時的確會嚮往當個海盜；而且，虎克單指名他讓他有點兒得意。

「我有一次曾想叫自己紅手約翰。」他怯怯地回答。

「不錯的名字。如果你加入我們，兄弟，在這裡，我們就會叫你這個稱號。」

「麥可，你覺得呢？」約翰問。

「如果我加入了，你們要怎麼稱呼我？」麥可詢問。

「黑鬍子喬。」

無疑地，這個稱號讓麥可印象深刻。「約翰，你說呢？」麥可希望約翰做決定，而約翰也希望對方做決定。

「我們加入後，仍效忠英國皇家嗎？」約翰又問。

虎克從齒縫中哼出答案：「你們應該要發誓，『去他的皇室。』」

「那麼我拒絕。」他叫道，重重地敲了虎克面前的酒桶一下。

「我也拒絕。」麥可也叫道。

「不列顛帝國萬歲！」柯利尖叫。

狂怒的海盜摀了他們的嘴，虎克怒吼道：「你們的命運就這樣決定了，把他們的母親帶上來，準備好舷板。」

這些男孩只不過是孩子，當他們看到喬克及西科準備走舷板，臉色都不禁發白。

但溫蒂被帶上來時，他們都努力喬裝鎮定勇敢。

對孩子來說，海盜彼此之間的稱號至少仍有一股吸引力，但在溫蒂眼中，她只看到這艘海盜船有好久沒打掃了。船舷每一面窗上的玻璃都沾滿了灰塵，足以讓你在上面用手指頭寫下「骯髒的豬」；溫蒂已經寫了好幾遍了。看著孩子們圍繞在身邊，她卻仍想不出解救他們的方法。

「嘿，小美人兒，」虎克的聲音像摻了蜜，「妳等著看自己的孩子落水吧。」

「他們要死了？」溫蒂問，臉上帶著一種非常輕蔑的神色，讓虎克看了幾乎氣得發昏。

「沒錯！」虎克咆哮道。「全部給我安靜，」他威風八面地說，「聽聽母親和孩子們訣別吧。」

此時的溫蒂充滿了高尚的情操。「親愛的孩子們，我要說最後幾句話，」她堅定地說，「我想，我要代你們真正的母親送你們一句話，就是：『我們希望自己的孩子像個英國紳士般莊嚴地死去。』」

即使是海盜，也不禁為之敬畏。托托歇斯底里地叫了起來：「我要遵照母親的希望行動。尼伯斯，你呢？」

「當然是依照母親的希望。雙胞胎，你們呢？」

「照著母親的話。約翰，你——」

不過，虎克再度開口了。

「把溫蒂綁起來。」他怒吼。

史密將溫蒂綁到船桅上。「看這裡，親愛的，」史密低語道，「如果妳答應當我的母親，我就救妳。」

但即便是史密，溫蒂也無法答應。「我寧可沒有任何孩子，也不要你。」她驕傲地說。

令人難過的是，當史密將溫蒂綁在船桅上時，竟然沒有一個孩子注意她，所有人的眼光都放在舷板上。想到要在這塊木板上走完人生最後一小段路，他們就再也沒辦法奢望保持男子氣概。他們的思考能力消失了，只能呆呆地看著木板，不停發抖。

虎克咬著牙對他們微笑，隨後走向溫蒂。他想要讓溫蒂轉過臉來，好看見孩子一個接一個走在刑板上。但是，他卻永遠沒辦法碰到溫蒂，也永遠沒辦法聽見他想聽到的痛苦叫聲；相反地，他聽到了另一個聲音。

那是鱷魚恐怖的滴答滴答聲。

「把我藏起來。」他啞著嗓子說。

海盜把他圍了起來，他們全移開視線，不想見到那隻即將爬上船的生物。他們沒想過要與那隻鱷魚爭鬥，這是宿命。

虎克藏起來後，孩子們便好奇地衝到船邊，想看看爬上船的鱷魚。此時，這個夜晚最讓他們詫異的事發生了：前來拯救他們的不是鱷魚，而是彼得潘。

彼得潘示意他們不要發出高興的叫聲，以免引起懷疑。接著，他就繼續發出滴滴答答的聲音前進。

第十四章 決一生死

我們最後一次看到彼得潘時，他正一隻手指按在唇上，一手按著刀，悄悄地走過夢幻島。他看見鱷魚經過時，起先並不覺得牠有什麼特別，但隨後就想起來，鱷魚肚子裡的滴答聲一直沒出現。起初，他還覺得有點兒古怪，但隨即得到結論，時鐘已經停止運轉了。

彼得潘無暇顧慮鱷魚忽然失去親密夥伴的感受，開始盤算如何利用這個變故。最後，他決定發出滴答滴答的聲音，讓野蠻的海盜以為他是隻鱷魚，這樣就能輕鬆地混進去。他模仿得很好，但卻造成了一個無法預料的結果──鱷魚也聽到了滴答聲，所以就跟著他。

彼得潘毫無困難地抵達岸邊，繼續向前邁進。他的腿自然而然地在水裡游了起來，似乎沒發現已經進入另一種自然元素中。彼得潘在游泳時，心中只有一個念頭：

「這一回，我要跟虎克一決生死。」他已經滴答滴答地說了好久，所以現在也渾然不覺地發出這個聲音。

相反地，彼得潘還以爲自己像隻老鼠般無聲無息地溜到了船上呢。他很訝異地發現，海盜都離他遠遠的，被圍在中間的虎克則像聽到了鱷魚似地嚇個半死。

鱷魚！一想到鱷魚，不消多久，彼得潘就想到了自己的滴答聲。一開始，他還以爲這聲音是鱷魚發出來的，所以迅速轉過頭查看。接著，他就明白聲音是自己發出來的，眞相於焉大白。「我眞聰明啊。」他馬上就這麼想，並向男孩們示意別鼓掌。

此時，舵手艾德泰奈特正好從船艙出來，走上了甲板。彼得潘準確地攻擊海盜，約翰隨即用手摀住那個不幸傢伙的嘴，以防他發出臨死的呻吟。海盜往前栽下去，四個男孩趕緊抓住他，免得他撲倒的聲音太過大聲。彼得潘打了個手勢，於是他們將屍體丟入海裡。水花濺了一下，一切又恢復平靜。

沒有多久，彼得潘就躡手躡腳地溜到小船艙裡。海盜開始鼓起勇氣到處巡視，他們現在可以聽見彼此驚惶的喘息聲，這表示那個恐怖的聲音已經消失了。

「船長，鱷魚離開了。」史密擦擦眼鏡說，「一切都沒事了。」

虎克慢慢地從衣領中抬起頭來，注意地傾聽，想知道四周還有沒有滴答滴答的回音。眞的沒有聲音了，於是他振起精神，挺直身子。

「那麼，讓孩子開始走舷板吧。」虎克無恥地嚷道。因為男孩看到了他狼狽害怕的模樣，所以他此刻益發憎恨他們。

為了讓這些孩子更加害怕，開始在想像出來的跳板上跳舞，邊做鬼臉邊對他們唱歌。歌唱完後，他說：「你們走跳板之前，想不想試試鞭子的滋味啊？」

所有的孩子都跪了下來。「不要，不要。」他們可憐地哀求道，所有的海盜都忍不住笑了。

「喬克，把九尾鞭拿來，」虎克說，「那玩意兒放在船艙裡。」

船艙！彼得潘就在船艙裡！孩子們互相凝視。

「是，是。」喬克爽快地答道，走進船艙。孩子們的眼光追隨著他。

船艙內忽然傳來一陣淒厲的慘叫，歌聲嘎然中止。這一聲尖叫響徹整艘船，然後又傳來一聲歡呼——孩子們相當清楚這是什麼聲音，但那些海盜都膽怯起來。

「那是什麼聲音？」虎克問道。

義大利籍的西科躊躇一會兒，便進入船艙。之後，他蹣跚地走出來，神色陰鬱。

第十四章　決一生死

「笨狗，比爾喬克怎麼了？」虎克高高在上，不滿地說道。

「他死了，被刀刺死的。」西科的聲音聽來虛渺空洞。

「比爾喬克死了！」海盜全都吃驚地叫了起來。

「西科，」虎克以無情的口吻下令，「去船艙把那個騙子給我抓來。」

西科是最勇敢的海盜，此刻卻跪倒在船長面前叫道：「不，不要。」然而，虎克威脅地舉起鐵爪。

西科認命地舉起雙手，走去船艙。這回，沒有人唱歌，大家全都專注地聆聽。同樣地，又傳來一聲淒厲的叫聲和歡呼聲。

虎克打了一個手勢，集合他的部下。「豈有此理。」他氣憤地說，「誰幫我去抓那個混蛋過來？」

「你是說你想去吧，西科？」他故意若有所思地說。

「等西科出來之後再說吧。」史塔基吼道，其他人也都附和他。

「我想，我聽到你自告奮勇喔，史塔基。」虎克不懷好意地說。

「不，我對天發誓，並沒有！」史塔基叫道。

「我的鐵爪聽到你是這麼說的，」虎克走向他，說，「史塔基，我想，跟鐵鉤開玩笑可是很不明智的。」

「要我進去，我寧願上吊。」史塔基頑強地說，其他人也都支持他。

「這是叛變嗎？」虎克異常快樂地說，「由史塔基主謀？」

「船長，求求你大發慈悲。」史塔基嗚咽著說，渾身發抖。

「史塔基，握個手吧。」虎克說完，伸出鐵鉤手。

史塔基望著四周求援，但大家全都背棄他。他背對著虎克往後走，眼裡佈滿紅色的血絲。之後，他發出一聲絕望的叫聲，就跳上長程砲，躍入海裡。

「那麼，現在，」虎克禮貌地詢問，「還有哪位仁兄想反抗嗎？」他提起一盞燈籠，舉起鐵鉤邪惡地揮了一下說，「讓我親自去抓出那個騙子。」說完，他就迅速地走進船艙。

虎克突然跟蹌地走了出來，手上的燈籠不見了。

「有個東西把燭光吹熄了。」虎克的聲音有點兒顫抖。

「西科怎麼了？」努得問。

「跟喬克一樣死了。」虎克簡短地說明。

虎克不願再回船艙的態度讓所有人大感意外，反抗的聲音再起。海盜都很迷信，庫克森就嚷道：「人家說，船上若多了一個來歷不明的人，就注定要倒楣。」

「有人說，」另一個人惡毒地看著虎克，說道，「他出現時，會化身為船上最邪惡的男人。」

「船長，他有鐵爪嗎？」庫克森無禮地問，隨後他們一個一個都叫了起來。「這艘船受到詛咒了。」聽到這裡，孩子們忍不住發出歡呼。虎克本來幾乎忘了這些孩子的存在，他回過頭看見他們，臉色立刻發亮。

「夥計，」虎克對部下叫道，「我有個主意。我們打開艙門，把這些囚犯趕進去，讓他們去跟那個怪物拚命。如果他們殺了怪物，那最好；如果怪物殺了他們，我們也沒有損失。」

這是海盜最後一次欽佩虎克，他們忠誠地執行他的命令。男孩們假裝掙扎了一下，就被推到船艙裡，艙門也關上了。

「現在，注意聽。」虎克叫道。所有人都專心地傾聽，卻沒有人敢面向艙門。是的，除了一個人——一直被綁在船桅上的溫蒂。她期待的結果不是慘叫，也不是歡呼，而是彼得潘出現。

她的期盼沒多久就實現了。彼得潘在船艙裡發現了他所要找的東西：孩子們手鏽的鑰匙。然後，孩子紛紛拿起他們所能找到的武器，悄悄地溜出船艙。彼得潘示意他們藏起來，就跑去砍斷縛住溫蒂的繩子，接下來應該沒有什麼事會比他們一起飛離這艘船更簡單了；然而，彼得潘的誓言：「這一回我要跟虎克一決生死。」攔阻了他們。所以，彼得放溫蒂自由後，便低聲要她跟其他人一起藏起來，他自己則取代溫蒂站在船桅前，身上還穿著溫蒂的外套喬扮成她。然後，彼得潘深吸一口氣，便發出一聲歡呼。

海盜以為這聲歡呼代表著船艙裡的孩子都被殺死了，不禁驚慌失措。虎克試著安撫他們，但沒有用，這群走狗就像野狗一樣露出尖牙。

「夥計，」虎克準備要誘騙部下，或是使用武力來對付他們——無論如何，他可一點兒都不畏懼——他說：「我知道了，這都是因為船上有個不吉利的人。」

「對，」所有人都哼了一聲說，「就是那個有鐵鉤的男人。」

「不，不是的，夥計，不是的，是個女孩。一個女孩出現在海盜船上，從來就不是件好事。如果她消失的話，我們就會沒事了。」

他們有些人想起，夫林特也曾這麼說過。「值得一試。」他們帶點猶疑回應。

「把那個女孩丟入水裡。」虎克命令，於是海盜們衝向船桅上穿著外套的人形。

「小姐，現在沒人可以救妳了。」穆林斯揶揄地說。

「有一個人可以。」那個身影回答。

「誰？」

「復仇者彼得潘！」可怕的回答！彼得潘說完，就扔開他的外套。海盜們恍然大悟，原來在船艙裡搞怪的就是彼得潘。

最後，虎克狂暴地怒吼道，「將彼得潘大卸八塊！」但他的自信已經完全喪失了。

「上啊，男孩們，打倒海盜。」彼得潘嚷道。下一秒鐘，兵刀相接的聲音立刻響遍了整艘船。海盜們很強壯，不過孩子們在戰鬥中更聰明。有些海盜跳入海裡，有的則躲入暗處，但都被史萊特利找出來，他沒有參與攻擊，只是拿著一盞燈籠跑來跑去，一發現海盜，就舉起燈籠往他們臉上照，讓他們的眼睛因強光看不清楚，而輕易成為男孩的刀下亡魂。

最後只剩下虎克了，孩子們包圍住他。他們逐步逼近他，虎克則抓住一個孩子當人質，一次又一次地殺出重圍。這時，另一個男孩剛殺死穆林斯，急急忙忙地衝過來加入這場戰局。

「收起你們的刀子，」剛加入的人嚷道，「這個人交給我。」

　第十四章　決一生死

虎克驀然發現，跟自己面對面的正是彼得潘。其他人都往後退，在他倆周圍圍成一圈。

有好長一段時間，這兩個敵人只是互相凝視對方。虎克微微地發抖，彼得潘臉上則露出奇異的笑容。

「所以，潘，」虎克終於開口了，「這全都是你搞的鬼。」

「沒錯，詹姆斯·虎克，」彼得潘堅定地答道，「都是我做的。」

「你這驕傲自大的小鬼，」虎克說，「準備受死吧。」

「你這邪惡陰沉的傢伙，」彼得潘回答，「你完蛋了。」

接下來雙方展開一場激烈的劍戰，在這期間男人和男孩勇敢地戰鬥。虎克頓時想拿出巴貝鳩許久以前在里歐教他的絕活，突然給敵人來個致命的一擊，結束一切。

但彼得潘卻能夠彎著身子在鐵鉤之下亂跑，猛烈地展開突擊，最後還刺中了虎克的肋骨。看到自己流血——記得嗎？我們說過那個血液的顏色很特別——虎克不禁嚇到了，他手中的劍掉落於地，只能任由彼得潘擺佈。

「就是現在！」其他的男孩子都嚷了起來，但彼得潘卻打了個高尚的手勢要對手拾起劍。虎克立刻照辦了，但心中卻有種悲哀的感覺，彼得潘真的很有禮貌。

迄今，虎克一直覺得和自己對戰的是個惡魔，但到了此刻，他心中卻出現了更可怕的猜疑。

「潘，你到底是誰？」虎克啞著嗓子問。

「我是青春，我是歡樂，」彼得潘胡亂回答道，「我是剛破蛋而出的幼鳥。」

當然，這不過是胡言亂語；但對憂鬱的虎克來說，這些話證明了彼得潘對自己並不會過於在意，這樣的不經意正是禮儀的極致。

「受死吧。」虎克絕望地喊道。

虎克宛若一台打穀機，開始狂亂地攻擊，他的每一刀都可以殺掉兩個上前阻撓的人，但彼得潘卻安然無事地在他身邊晃來晃去，好像虎克揮舞刀子時所撼動的風將他吹出了危險區域。彼得潘還不時鑽進空隙，發動刺擊。

虎克現在充滿了絕望，這個易怒的男人對生命已不再戀棧，只盼望一件事：在死之前，可以看到彼得潘失禮。

他停止戰鬥，衝進火藥庫，放了一把火。

「兩分鐘以內，」虎克叫道，「這艘船就會炸成灰燼。」

但彼得潘卻馬上從火藥庫中取出炸藥，不慌不忙地將炸藥丟入海裡。

虎克本身又有什麼反應呢？他搖搖晃晃地走上甲板，其他的男孩子開始圍攻他，

他徒勞地反擊，但他的心早就不在他們身上了。

虎克看到彼得潘握著一把匕首，從空中緩緩地飛向自己，於是就跳上船舷，躍入海中。他萬萬沒想到，鱷魚正在海裡面等著他。

這便是詹姆斯・虎克的結局。

隨著戰鬥結束，溫蒂從下面的船艙出來。溫蒂公平地稱讚每個人，當麥可指出他殺人的地方時，她還高興得顫抖。隨後，她領著他們進入虎克的艙房，指了指虎克掛在牆釘上的手錶，它正指著「一點半」呢！

最後一段時間發生的事，可以說是最重要的。你可以想見，溫蒂會多麼迅速地將孩子安置在海盜的床上，不過彼得潘例外。彼得潘在甲板上昂首闊步，直到最後才坐在長程砲旁睡著了。那個晚上，他又做了個夢，在夢中不停地哭喊，溫蒂一直將他緊緊地摟在懷中。

第十五章　回家

育兒室唯一的變化是，清晨九點到晚上六點時，那裡已經沒有狗窩了。孩子走後，達林先生非常自責，認為都是自己綁住娜娜造成的，他覺得娜娜其實自始至終都比自己聰明。

他在痛苦悔恨之中發誓，除非孩子回來，否則他不會離開狗屋。

達林先生對娜娜的敬意相當令人感動。他不讓娜娜進狗屋，但其他事情他全都順著娜娜。

每天早上，達林先生就坐在狗屋裡，讓車子連同狗屋一道載到辦公室，然後在傍晚六點以同樣的方式回家。若我們還記得達林先生曾經多在乎鄰居的眼光，就可以知道達林先生此時表現得多堅強，他現在的一舉一動可都會引起鄰居詫異的目光哩。

這行動或許有點不切實際，但卻是相當莊嚴的。很快地，這件事的內幕就傳開來，大家都深受感動。

達林太太坐在育兒室裡等著喬治達林返家，她的眼裡盡是憂傷。坐在椅子裡的她已經睡著了。她的手不停地撫著胸口，好像那裡很痛似地。達林太太突然驚醒，呼喚孩子的名字：但除了娜娜，房內空無一人。

「噢，娜娜，我夢到我的寶貝回來了。」

娜娜雙眼模糊，但牠只能將腳掌輕輕地放在痛苦的達林太太的膝部。她們一起坐著，等待達林先生跟狗屋回家。當達林先生探出頭來親吻太太時，我們可以看到，他的臉比過去更加疲憊，但臉上的表情柔和多了。

社交上的成功並沒有讓達林先生恃寵而驕，相反地，他變得更加親切。有時，他會半坐在狗屋外，與達林太太討論這些成功，當達林太太說她希望他別因此而改變為人時，他按按她的手，請她放心。

「妳彈琴幫我入眠，好嗎？」他問。達林太太走過去時，達林先生不假思索地說：「關上那扇窗。我覺得起風了。」

「天啊，喬治，千萬別要我這麼做，這扇窗一定得隨時為孩子們敞開。隨時都要，隨時都要。」

這回就換達林先生求她原諒了。達林太太走進孩子白天時的遊戲室消遣，達林先生則睡著了；他睡著時，彼得潘和叮噹貝爾飛了進來。

「叮噹，快點，」彼得潘低聲道，「關上窗子，栓上它。沒錯。現在，我們從前門離開。這樣溫蒂回來時，就會以為她的母親把她擋在窗外了，她只得跟我一起回夢幻島。」

彼得潘一點兒也不覺得自己的行為卑鄙，相反地，他開心地跳起舞來。他又偷偷望進遊戲室裡，想看看誰正在彈琴。他對婷克低語：「那是溫蒂的媽媽！」

他再次探頭窺看，發現歌聲乍然中止。達林太太的頭擱在一只箱子上，眼眶中含著淚水。

「她希望我能夠打開窗戶，」彼得潘想著，「但我偏不，我不要。」

他又繼續偷看，淚水仍在那裡，又湧上了更多淚水。

「她真的好愛溫蒂。」彼得潘自言自語道。他開始對達林太太生起氣來，不明白為什麼她不可以沒有溫蒂。

我也需要她！彼得潘想大喊。**我們不能同時擁有她。**

他不再看她，但卻甩不開達林太太的影子。就算他開始四處跳躍，不停扮鬼臉，但只要一停下來，她就好像會出現在他身體裡，扣著他的心。

「噢，好吧。」他尖叫，對自然的法則嗤之以鼻道，「我們不想再看到愚蠢的母親了。」接下來，他就飛走了。

所以，最後溫蒂、約翰和麥可回到家時，發現窗戶還是敞開的——這實在不是他們應得的待遇。他們一點也不覺得羞恥地落到地板上，最小的麥可早就忘記自己的家是什麼模樣了。

「我的天啊。」約翰叫道，「看看這個狗屋！」他衝向它。

「娜娜或許在裡頭。」溫蒂說。

但約翰吹了聲口哨。「各位，」他說，「裡面有個人呢。」

「是爸爸！」溫蒂叫了起來。

「讓我看看爸爸。」麥可殷殷請求，然後好好瞧了瞧。「他沒有我殺死的海盜那麼高大。」他失望的模樣真讓人慶幸達林先生睡著了，如果他聽到小麥可說的那幾句話，一定會很難過。

溫蒂和約翰看到父親待在狗屋裡，不禁嚇得倒退幾步。

「想當然，」約翰像個對自己的記憶失去信心的人，說，「他這陣子不會是睡在狗屋吧？」

「約翰，」溫蒂結結巴巴地說，「或許，我們對過去的記憶沒有我們以為的那麼眞確。」

他們都覺得身體在發冷；呵，這眞是活該。

「母親眞是疏忽，」小無賴約翰還說，「我們回來了，她竟然不在這裡迎接我們。」

此時，達林太太又開始彈起琴來。

「是媽媽，」溫蒂叫道，去遊戲室偷看。

「正是她沒錯！」約翰說。

「所以，溫蒂妳不是我們眞正的母親囉？」很想睡覺的麥可問道。

「噢，天啊！」溫蒂第一次覺得良心因悔恨而刺痛，她叫了起來，「我們回來得太晚了。」

「我們偷偷爬進去，」約翰提議，「用手蒙住媽媽的眼睛。」

但溫蒂覺得他們應該用更溫和的方式公佈這個好消息，她心生一計。

「我們都回到他們自己的床上躺著等母親進來，就好像我們從未離開過。」

晨星事業群
晨星出版有限公司

407台中市工業區30路1號

No.1, Gongyequ 30th Rd., Xitun Dist., Taichung City 407, Taiwan

Tel：+886-2359-5820 | Fax：+886-2355-0581

E-mail：service@morningstar.com.tw

Website：www.morningstar.com.tw

-------------------- 請沿虛線對摺裝訂，謝謝！ --------------------

寄件人姓名：_____

E-mail：_____

地址：_____(郵遞區號)_____市/縣_____鄉/鎮/市/區

_____路/街____段____巷____弄____號____樓/室

電話：住宅（   ）_____ 公司（   ）_____

手機_____

搜尋 / 晨星奇幻

加入晨星奇幻官方FB，掌握第一手最新資訊，優質作品訊息不漏接

親愛的讀者：

感謝你購買本書。歡迎你購書／閱讀完畢以後，寫下想給編輯部的意見，本回函免貼郵資。如有心得／插圖佳作，將會刊登於晨星奇幻粉絲團上。填妥個人資料後，除了不定期會收到「晨星閱讀專刊」外，我們也將於每月抽出幸運讀者，贈送新書或獨家贈品。

★購買的書是：＿＿＿＿＿＿＿＿＿＿＿＿＿＿＿＿＿＿＿＿＿＿＿＿＿

★姓名：＿＿＿＿＿＿　★性別：□男 □女　★生日：西元＿＿＿年＿＿＿月＿＿＿日

★職業：□學生／就讀學校：＿＿＿＿＿＿＿　□老師／任教學校：＿＿＿＿＿＿

　　　　□服務 □製造 □資訊 □軍公教 □金融 □傳播 □其他＿＿＿＿＿

★本書中最吸引您的是哪一篇文章或哪一段話呢？＿＿＿＿＿＿＿＿＿＿＿

★吸引您購買此書的原因？

　　□於＿＿＿＿＿＿（網路）書店發掘新知時　□看＿＿＿＿＿＿報紙／雜誌時瞄到

　　□＿＿＿＿＿＿電台 DJ 熱情推薦　□親朋好友拍胸脯保證　□受海報或文案吸引

　　□各大書店電子報　□晨星奇幻粉絲團介紹　□看＿＿＿＿＿＿部落格版主推薦

　　□其他令人意想不到的奇妙緣分：＿＿＿＿＿＿＿＿＿＿＿＿＿＿＿＿＿

★對於本書的評分？（請填代號：①非常滿意 ②還不錯 ③尚可 ④尚需改進）

　　封面設計＿＿＿＿＿　版面編排＿＿＿＿＿　內容＿＿＿＿＿　文／譯筆＿＿＿＿＿

★你希望晨星能出版哪些類型的兒童或青少年書籍？（複選）

　　□奇幻冒險 □勵志故事 □幽默故事 □推理故事 □藝術人文

　　□中外經典名著 □自然科學與環境教育 □漫畫 □其他＿＿＿＿＿＿

★您對本書的建議或任何想法：

所以，當達林太太進入育兒室，想看看丈夫是否睡著時，卻發現每張床上都睡了人。他們從床上跳了起來，尖叫著跑去擁抱他們的母親。

「喬治，喬治。」達林太太終於能再開口說話時，立刻喚醒她的丈夫；達林先生醒過來，分享了她的喜悅，娜娜也衝了進來。再沒有比這個場景更可愛的畫面了：可惜，除了一個在窗戶旁邊偷看的男孩外，沒有其他人看到這個景象。彼得潘擁有許多其他孩子無法了解的快樂，但是，他此刻透過窗戶所看到的喜悅畫面，是他永遠也無法得到的。

第十六章 溫蒂長大後

我希望你們會想要知道其他的男孩怎麼了。他們爬上樓梯，以為這樣可以給他們較好的印象。他們脫下帽子，在達林太太面前站成一列，心中可真希望自己穿的不是海盜衣裳。他們沒有說話，但眼神都在請求達林太太收留他們。他們也應該看看達林先生的，但他們忘記了。當然，達林太太立刻說她願意收留他們，但達林先生卻露出奇怪的沮喪神情。他們看得出來他正在考慮，他一定是覺得六個人太多了。

雙胞胎中的哥哥是個驕傲的人，於是他漲紅著臉表示：「先生，你覺得我們人數太多了嗎？如果是這樣，我們可以離開。」

「爸爸！」溫蒂憤怒地嚷起來。

「喬治！」達林太太嘆道，看到親愛的丈夫這樣小氣，真教她難受。

隨即，達林先生迸出淚來，真相於是大白。他說他跟達林太太一樣樂意收留他們，但他覺得他們應該也要問問他的意見，而不是將他當個無足輕重的人。

「我不覺得他是無足輕重的人。」托托立刻回答，「柯利，你覺得他是無足輕重的人嗎？」

「不，我不這麼認為。史萊特利，你覺得他無足輕重嗎？」

「當然不。雙胞胎，你們覺得呢？」

最後發現，沒有人覺得達林先生無足輕重。達林先生因此非常開心，他說如果孩子們不介意，他就把他們安置在客廳裡。

「我們會很舒適的，先生。」他們向他保證。

「現在，跟著你們的首領。」達林先生高興地叫道。

於是達林先生跳著舞離開，其他人也都尾隨著他跳著舞找客廳去了，嘴邊還高喊

「萬歲！」。

至於彼得潘，他在離開之前，又見了溫蒂一次。他並沒有真的飛到窗戶邊，而是在飛行途中拂過窗戶，溫蒂若想見他，就可以打開窗戶叫他。

「哈囉，溫蒂，再見了。」彼得潘說。

「彼得潘，」溫蒂支支吾吾地道，「你想不想跟我父母說一說那件甜蜜的事情？」

達林太太走到窗邊，目光銳利地看著溫蒂。她對彼得潘說，她已經收養了其他男孩，也很樂意再多他一個。

「你會送我到學校唸書嗎？」彼得潘精明地問。

「會。」

「然後去工作？」

「我想是吧。」

「所以我很快就會變成一個大人？」

「是很快。」

「我不想去學校學一些嚴肅的東西，」彼得潘憤怒地說，「我不想長大。喔，溫蒂的媽媽，想想看我早晨醒來，發現自己滿臉鬍渣的模樣！」

「彼得潘，」溫蒂安撫他說，「就算你有鬍渣，我還是愛你。」達林太太向彼得潘伸出手，但他拒絕了。

「但你要住在哪裡呢？」

「跟叮噹一起住在我們為溫蒂蓋的房子。仙子晚上總是在樹梢睡覺，所以叮噹會把房子放到那裡。」

「多可愛啊。」溫蒂嚮往地叫起來，嚇得達林太太趕緊拉住她。

「我以爲所有的仙子都死了。」達林太太說。

「但一直有新的仙子誕生。」溫蒂解釋，她現在可是這方面的權威了，「新生的嬰兒第一次笑時，就會有一個小仙子誕生。他們住在樹梢上的巢裡，淡紫色模樣的是男孩，白色的是女孩，藍色的則是還弄不清性別的小傻蛋。」

「我的樂趣多得很呢。」彼得潘盯著溫蒂說道。

「到了傍晚，獨自一人坐在火爐邊就很寂寞了。」溫蒂說。

「我有叮噹作陪。」

「叮噹有很多事情做不來。」溫蒂有點狠毒地提醒他。

「好啊，那妳跟我一起回去。」

「媽媽，我可以去嗎？」

「當然不行。我好不容易等到妳回來，絕不會再讓妳離開了。」

「喔，算了。」彼得潘說，好像自己只是出於禮貌問問；但達林太太看到他的嘴角抽搐，就做了一個慷慨的決定：每年春天溫蒂可以回夢幻島一個禮拜，爲彼得潘大掃除。

溫蒂憂傷地說：「彼得潘，春天來臨之前，你不會忘了我吧？不會吧？」

彼得潘許下承諾，接著就飛走了。他把達林太太的吻帶走了——那個吻一直沒有人可以得到，但彼得潘卻輕易地得到了。這真有趣。達林太太看起來心滿意足。

所有的孩子理所當然都進了學校。他們上學不到一個禮拜，就非常後悔不該離開夢幻島，不過為時已晚。他們逐漸喪失了飛行能力。到後來，他們甚至連帽子飛走了，也無法飛過去追。原因是缺乏練習，他們說；但真正的原因其實是，他們都不再相信過去的歲月了。

儘管麥可一直被別的男孩取笑，但他對過去歲月的記憶比其他男孩深刻。所以，彼得潘第一年底回來接溫蒂時，他也跟溫蒂一起回夢幻島。溫蒂身上所穿的工作服，是她在夢幻島時利用樹葉和野莓果縫製而成的，她很擔心彼得潘會注意到那件衣服已經變得很小了；但彼得潘並沒有注意到，他有太多事要說了。

溫蒂一直期待能夠與彼得潘敘敘往事，但彼得潘的心思已被新的冒險佔滿了。

「誰是虎克船長？」溫蒂提到那個狡猾的敵人時，彼得潘頗富興味地問道。

「你不記得啦？」溫蒂吃驚地問。

「我殺了他們之後就忘記了。」彼得潘滿不在乎地回答。

當溫蒂說她希望叮噹貝爾見到她會很高興時，彼得潘又說：「誰是叮噹貝爾？」

「噢，彼得潘。」溫蒂驚訝到了極點。但就算她試著解釋，彼得潘還是想不起來。

溫蒂很難過地發現，去年對彼得潘來說只不過是昨日罷了，但對溫蒂來說，這一年的等待卻是那麼漫長。

翌年，彼得潘並沒有來找溫蒂。那套舊的工作服已經不合身了，溫蒂換上新的工作服等候彼得潘。但是，他並沒有出現。

「或許他生病了。」麥可說。

「你知道他不生病的。」

麥可走近溫蒂，顫抖地低聲說道：「溫蒂，或許從來沒有這個人！」若不是麥可接著就哭了起來，溫蒂也一定會哭出來。

再隔一年的春季打掃時光，彼得潘來了。奇怪的是，他一直不知道自己漏了一年。這次是溫蒂最後一次看到他。他們再次相遇時，溫蒂已嫁為人婦，此時，彼得潘對她來說，不過就是幼年玩具箱裡的一粒塵埃。溫蒂長大了。你不必為她感到遺憾，她是那種喜歡長大的人之一。最後，她還依著自己的意願，比其他女孩早一天長大。

此時，所有的男孩都長大了，行為也都恰如其分。

溫蒂穿著潔白飾有粉紅色緞帶的禮服出嫁。還真是奇怪，彼得潘竟沒有飛到教堂阻止婚禮。年華如流水，溫蒂生了一個女兒。這個女娃娃叫珍。

現在，育兒室裡只有兩張床，分別是珍及保姆的。娜娜死了，狗屋也消失了。

珍的保母每週會有一天晚上外出，所以，此時哄珍睡覺就成了溫蒂的責任。這是她們說故事的時光。珍喜歡將床單蒙住自己與母親，假裝蓋一個帳棚，然後在黑暗中低聲說：「妳現在看到什麼了？」

「我今晚什麼也沒看見。」溫蒂說，心想如果娜娜在場，一定會禁止她們談論這個話題。

「有，妳有看到。」珍說，「妳還是個小女孩時，看得見。」

「寶貝，那是好久以前的事情了，」溫蒂嘆息，「天啊，時間飛逝哪！」

「時間飛的方式，」精明的珍問，「跟妳過去飛的方式一樣嗎？」

「我飛的方式！珍，妳知道嗎？我有時都懷疑自己以前是否真的會飛。」

「媽咪，為什麼妳現在不能飛了？」

「親愛的，因為我長大了。人長大以後，就會忘了飛行的方法。」

第十六章　溫蒂長大後

「為什麼會忘記？」

「因為他們不再歡樂純真、不再無憂無慮了，只有歡樂純真、無憂無慮的孩子才會飛。」

「什麼是歡樂純真、無憂無慮？我希望我也是這樣。」或許，溫蒂得承認，她領悟了一些事情。

「我相信，」溫蒂說，「一切都跟這間育兒室有關。」

「我也如此相信，」珍說，「繼續說吧。」

於是，她們從彼得潘飛進來找影子那晚開始說起。

「後來，他帶我們飛往夢幻島，那裡有仙子、海盜、印地安人及珊瑚湖，還有地底之家及小屋子。」

「彼得潘最後對妳說的話是什麼？」

「他對我說的最後一句話是：『要永遠記得我，那在晚上妳就可以聽到我的歡呼聲。』」

「沒錯。」

「但，天啊，他完完全全忘了我了。」溫蒂微笑著說。她已經長大，能釋懷了。

「他歡呼的聲音是怎樣呢？」珍已經問了一個晚上了。

「像這樣。」溫蒂試著模仿彼得潘的叫聲。

「不對，不是這樣。」珍認真的說，「是像這樣。」她學得比母親還要像。

溫蒂有點詫異地說：「親愛的，你怎麼知道的？」

「我睡覺時，經常會聽到他的歡呼聲。」珍回答。

「噢，沒錯，很多女孩睡覺時都會聽到這個聲音，但我是唯一醒著聽到的人。」

「你真幸運。」珍說。

之後一個晚上，悲劇發生了。那時是春季，當天晚上的故事時間已過，珍在床上睡著了。溫蒂坐在地板上，她靠近火爐，好看清手中的針線活兒，育兒室裡其他地方都一片黑暗。當她坐著縫補衣服時，聽到了一聲歡呼。接著，窗戶像過去一樣被風吹開了，彼得潘跳了進來。

彼得潘跟過去看來一模一樣，溫蒂立刻發現他仍然還沒有換牙。彼得潘還是個小男孩，但溫蒂已經長大了。她在火爐旁蜷縮成一團，不敢移動，感到無助又罪惡，她竟然長大了。

「哈囉，溫蒂。」彼得潘對她打招呼，並沒有注意到有什麼不同，他向來想的都是自己的事情。況且，在微弱的光線中，溫蒂身上的白洋裝看來就跟他們初次見面時穿的白色睡袍一樣。

彼得潘看著床。「哈囉，那是新出現的人？」

「沒錯。」

「男孩還是女孩？」

「女孩。」

「彼得潘，」溫蒂支支吾吾地問，「你還希望我跟你一起飛走嗎？」

「當然囉，這就是我出現的目的啊。」彼得潘有點不悅地說道，「妳忘記現在是春季的大掃除時間嗎？」

溫蒂知道，就算告訴彼得潘他已經錯失了好多個春季打掃時光，也是於事無補。

「我不能去，」溫蒂帶著歉意說：「我已經忘記怎麼飛了。」

溫蒂終於站了起來，現在，一陣恐懼遍佈彼得潘全身。「怎麼一回事？」彼得潘發著抖叫道。

「怎麼一回事？」他又問了一遍。

溫蒂必須吐露一切。「我老了，彼得潘，我已經有二十好幾了。我好久以前就長大了。」

「妳答應過妳不會長大的！」

「我沒辦法啊。彼得潘，我結婚了。」

「不，妳騙人。」

「我沒騙人，床上那個小女孩是我的孩子。」

「不，她不是。」

但彼得潘還是認為她應該是溫蒂的小孩，所以他舉起手中的匕首，走向熟睡中的孩子。他沒有攻擊她，相反地，他跌坐在地板上，開始啜泣。雖然，溫蒂過去能夠輕易地安撫彼得潘，但此刻她卻不知該從何安慰起。

彼得潘繼續哭著，他的啜泣聲一下子就吵醒了珍。珍在床上坐起身，立刻很好奇地看著一切。

當溫蒂回房時，彼得潘已經坐在床腳高興地歡呼了，珍則穿著睡袍欣喜若狂地在房內飛舞。

「再見了。」彼得潘對溫蒂說，隨後就飛向空中，天真的珍也跟著飛到他身旁；

對珍來說，飛行已經是最簡單的移動方式。

溫蒂衝到窗戶旁。

「不，不要。」溫蒂尖叫。

「只有春季的打掃時光，」珍說，「彼得潘希望我幫他春季大掃除。」

「我多想跟你們一起去啊。」溫蒂嘆息道。

「妳知道妳沒法子飛了。」珍說。

最後，溫蒂讓他們一起飛走了。我們最後看了她一眼，她正站在窗戶旁，看著彼得潘與珍沒入天際，逐漸變成星子般的大小。

你現在看到溫蒂，會發現她的頭髮已經花白，身體也縮小了，畢竟，這個故事是好久以前的事了。珍現在也長大成為一個平凡的人，生了個女兒叫瑪格麗特。到了春天的打掃時光，除非彼得潘忘記，否則他都會來找瑪格麗特，帶她到夢幻島，聽她講述他自己的故事，還聽得津津有味。等到瑪格麗特長大後，她也會有個女兒，這個女兒也會變成彼得潘的母親。只要孩子一直是歡樂純真、無憂無慮的，這個故事就會永遠繼續下去。

PETER PAN

All children, except one,
grow up.

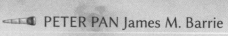

PETER PAN James M. Barrie

CONTENTS

CHAPTER 1

PETER BREAKS THROUGH

All children, except one, grow up. Wendy learned this when she was playing in a garden at the age of two. She plucked another flower and ran to her mother. Mrs. Darling hugged her and said, "Oh, why can't you remain like this forever!" This was all that passed between them on the subject, but henceforth Wendy knew that she must grow up.

Of course they lived at 14, and until Wendy came her mother was the chief one. She was a lovely lady, with a romantic mind and such a sweet mocking mouth.

Mrs. Darling was married in white, and at first she kept the books perfectly, almost gleefully, as if it were a game, not so much as a Brussels sprout was missing; but by and by whole cauliflowers dropped out, and instead of them there were pictures of babies without faces.

Wendy came first, then John, then Michael.

Mrs. Darling loved to have everything just so, and Mr.

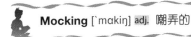

Mocking [ˋmɑkɪŋ] adj. 嘲弄的

Darling had a passion for being exactly like his neighbours; so, of course, they had a nurse. As they were poor, owing to the amount of milk the children drank, this nurse was a prim Newfoundland dog, called Nana, who had belonged to no one in particular until the Darlings engaged her. She had always considered children important, however, and the Darlings had become acquainted with her in Kensington Gardens. She proved to be quite a treasure of a nurse. How thorough she was at bath-time, and up at any moment of the night if one of her charges made the slightest cry. Of course her kennel was in the nursery. She had a genius for knowing when a cough is a thing to have no patience with and when it needs stocking round your neck. It was a lesson in of etiquette to see her escorting the children to school, walking sedately by their side when they were well behaved, and butting them back into line if they strayed.

No nursery could possibly have been conducted more correctly, and Mr. Darling knew it, yet he sometimes wondered uneasily whether the neighbours talked.

Prim [prɪm] adj. 一絲不苟、整齊
Kennel [ˋkɛn!] n. 狗屋
Sedately [sɪˋdetlɪ] adv. 鎮定地

Conduct [kənˋdʌkt] v. 引導；帶領

He had his position in the city to consider.

Nana also troubled him in another way. Sometimes, he had a feeling that she did not admire him. "I know she admires you tremendously, George," Mrs. Darling would assure him, and then she would sign to the children to be specially nice to father. Lovely dances followed, in which the only other servant, Liza, was sometimes allowed to join. How small she looked in her long skirt and maid's cap, though she had sworn, that she would never see ten again. when the Darlings hired her.

There were no families simpler happier than the Darlings until the com-ing of Peter Pan.

Mrs. Darling first heard of Peter when she was tidying up her children's minds. It is the nightly custom of every good mother after her children are asleep. If minds are drawers , then the memories of children are underwear and socks that need to be neatly folded and put away.

There are zigzag lines on a map of a child's mind, just like your temperature on a card, and those are probably roads in the island, for the Neverland is always more or

---

Admire [əd`maɪr] adj. 尊敬、欽佩

Tremendously [trɪ`mɛndəslɪ] adv. 極其、非常

Zigzag [`zɪgzæg] adj. 之字形的；鋸齒形的

less an island, with astonishing splashes of colour here and there, and coral reefs and rakish-looking craft in the offing, and savages and lonely lairs, and gnomes who are mostly tailors, and caves through which a river runs, and princes with six elder brothers, and a hut fast going to decay, and one very small old lady with a hooked nose.

Every child's Neverland is slightly different. John lived in a boat turned upside down on the sands, Michael in a wigwam, Wendy in a house of leaves deftly sewn together. John had no friends, Michael had friends at night, and Wendy had a pet wolf forsaken by its parents.

Occasionally in the travels through children's minds, Mrs. Darling found things she could not understand, and of these quite the most perplexing was the word Peter.

"Who is this Peter?" she asked her daughter. "Is he a friend of yours?"

"Mother. Don't you remember him?"

At first Mrs. Darling did not know, but after thinking back into her childhood she just remembered a Peter Pan who was said to live with the fairies.

"But" she said to Wendy, "he would be grown up by this time."

Perplexing [pə`plɛksɪŋ] adj. 令人困惑的

"Oh no, he isn't grown up," Wendy assured con-fidently, "and he is just my size."

"I'm worried about this Peter Pan." Mrs. Darling consulted Mr. Darling, but he smiled pooh-pooh. "Mark my words," he said, "it is some nonsense Nana has been putting into their heads; just the sort of idea a dog would have. Leave it alone, and it will blow over."

But it would not blow over, and soon the troublesome boy gave Mrs. Darling quite a shock.

It was in this casual way that Wendy one morning made a disquieting revelation. Some leaves of a tree had been found on the nursery floor, which certainly were not there when the children went to bed, and Mrs. Darling was puzzling over them when Wendy said with smile:

"I do believe it is that Peter again!"

"Whatever do you mean, Wendy?"

"It's so naughty of him not to wipe," Wendy said, sighing. She was a tidy child.

She explained that Peter sometimes came to the nursery in the night and sat on the foot of her bed and played on his pipes to her.

"Sweetheart, No one can get into the house without knocking."

"I think he comes in by the window," she said.

"My love, it is three floors up. why did you not tell me of this before?"

"I forgot," said Wendy lightly. She was in a hurry to get her breakfast.

But, on the other hand, there were the leaves. Mrs. Darling examined them carefully; they were skeleton leaves, but she was sure they did not come from any tree that grew in England. She searched the room for other clues, but found none.

Certainly Wendy had been dreaming.

But Wendy had not been dreaming, as the very next night showed, the night on which the extraordinary adventures of these children have begun.

As all the children were once more in bed. It happened to be Nana's evening off, and Mrs. Darling had bathed them and sung to them till they had let go her hand and slid away into the land of sleep one by one.

All were looking so safe and cosy that she smiled at her fears now and she sat down tranquilly by the fire to sew.

Skeleton [ˈskɛlətn] adj. 骨骼

Cosy [ˈkozɪ] adj. 溫馨的

Tranquilly [ˈtræŋkwɪlɪ] adv. 平靜地

The fire was warm, however, and the nursery dimly lit by three night-lights, and presently the sewing lay on Mrs. Darling's lap. Then her head nodded, oh, so gracefully. She was asleep.

While she slept she had a dream. She dreamt that the Neverland had come too near and that a strange boy had broken through from it. But in her dream he had rent the film that obscures the Neverland, and she saw Wendy and John and Michael peeping through the gap.

The dream by itself would have been a trifle, but the window of the nursery blew open, while she was dreaming and a boy did drop on the floor. He was accompanied by a strange light, no bigger than a fist, which darted about the room like a living thing.

Mrs. Darling started up with a cry, and saw the boy, and somehow she knew at once that he was Peter Pan. He was a lovely boy, clad in skeleton leaves and the juices that ooze out of trees, but the most entrancing thing about him was that he had all his first teeth. When he saw she was a grown-up, he gnashed the little pearls at her.

Ooze [uz] v. 滲出

CHAPTER 2

THE SHADOW

Mrs. Darling screamed, and, as if in answer to a bell, the door opened, and Nana entered, returned from her evening out. She growled and sprang at the boy, who leapt lightly through the window. Again Mrs. Darling screamed, She didn't want the boy to die, and she ran down into the street to look for his little body, but it was not there; and she looked up, and in the black night she could see nothing but a shooting star, at least that's what she thought it was.

She returned to the nursery, and found Nana with something in her mouth, which proved to be the boy's shadow. As he leapt at the window Nana had closed it quickly, too late to catch him, but his shadow had not had time to get out; slam went the window and snapped it off.

Nana wanted to hang the shadow out the window, meaning "He is sure to come back for it; let us put it where he can get it easily without disturbing the children." But

Disturb [dɪˈstɜːb] v. 打擾、中斷

Mrs. Darling thought that it would look like laundry drying. Mr. Darling would be upset if the neighbors saw that.

She decided to roll the shadow up and put it away carefully in a drawer, until a fitting opportunity came for telling her husband.

The opportunity came a week later, on that never-to-be-forgotten Friday.

"I ought to have been specially careful on a Friday," she used to say afterwards to her husband, while perhaps Nana was on the other side of her, holding her hand.

"No, no," Mr. Darling always said, "I am responsible for it all."

They sat thus night after night recalling that fatal Friday, till every detail of it was stamped on their brains and came through on the other side like the faces on a bad coinage.

"If only I had not accepted that invitation to dine at 27," Mrs. Darling said. "If only I had not poured my medicine into Nana's bowl," said Mr. Darling.

"If only I had pretended to like the medicine," was what Nana's wet eyes said.

Opportunity [ˌɑpə-ˈtjunətɪ] n. 機會
Responsible [rɪˈspɑnsəb!] adj. 須負責任的
Stamp on [stæmpt ɑn] phr. 踩踏

Then one or more of them would break down altogether; Nana at the thought, "It's true, it's true, they ought not to have had a dog for a nurse." Many a time it was Mr. Darling who put the handkerchief to Nana's eyes.

They would sit there in the empty nursery, recalling fondly every smallest detail of that dreadful evening. It had begun so uneventfully, so precisely like a hundred other evenings, with Nana putting on the water for Michael's bath and carrying him to it on her back.

Then Mrs. Darling had come in, wearing her white evening-gown. She had dressed early because Wendy loved to see her in her evening-gown, with the necklace George had given her. She was wearing a braclet borrowed from Wendy. Wendy loved to lend her bracelet to her mother.

She had found her two older children playing at being herself and father on the occasion of Wendy's birth.

They go on with their recollections.

"It was then that I rushed in like a tornado, wasn't it?" Mr. Darling would say, scorning himself; and indeed he had been like a tornado.

Perhaps there was some excuse for him. He, too, had

Bracelet ['breslɪt] **n.** 手鐲

been dressing for the party, and all had gone well with him until he came to his tie.

This was such an occasion. He came rushing into the nursery with the crum pled little brute of a tie in his hand.

"Why, what is the matter, father dear?"

"Matter!" he yelled; he really yelled. "This tie, it will not tie."

He thought Mrs. Darling was not sufficiently impressed, and he went on sternly, "I warn you of this, mother, that unless this tie is round my neck we don't go out to dinner tonight, and if I don't go out to dinner tonight, I never go to the office again, and if I don't go to the office again, you and I starve, and our children will be flung into the streets."

Even then Mrs. Darling was placid, and with her nice cool hands she tied his tie for him, while the children stood around to see their fate decided. Mr. Darling thanked her carelessly, at once forgot his rage, and started dancing round the room with Michael on his back.

The romp had ended with the appearance of Nana, and most unluckily Mr. Darling collided against her, covering his trousers with dog hairs. The trousers was not only a new pair of trousers but also the first pair he had ever had with

Sufficiently [səˈfiʃəntlɪ] adv. 足夠地；充分地

braid, and he had to bite his lip to prevent the tears coming.
Of course Mrs. Darling brushed him, but he began to talk
again about its being a mistake to have a dog for a nurse.

"George, Nana is a treasure."

"No doubt, but I have an uneasy feeling at times that
she looks upon the children as puppies."

"Oh no, dear one, I feel sure she knows they have
souls."

"I wonder," Mr. Darling said thoughtfully, "I wonder."
It was an opportunity, his wife felt, for telling him about
the boy. At first he pooh-poohed the story, but he became
thoughtful when she showed him the shadow.

"It is nobody I know," he said, examining it carefully,
"but he does look a scoundrel."

"We were still discussing the shadow," says Mr. Darling,
"when Nana came in with Michael's medicine. You will
never carry the bottle in your mouth again, Nana, and it is
all my fault."

Strong man though he was, there is no doubt that Mr.
Darling had behaved rather foolishly over the medicine. If
he had a weakness, it was for thinking that all his life he had
taken medicine boldly, and so now, when Michael dodged

 Pooh-pooh [pu`pu] v. 嗤之以鼻；輕視

the spoon in Nana's mouth, he had said reprovingly, "Be a man, Michael."

"Won't; won't!" Michael cried naughtily. Mrs. Darling left the room to get a chocolate for him, and Mr. Darling thought this showed that Michael is in want of firmness.

"Mother, don't pamper him," he called after her. "Michael, when I was your age I took medicine without a murmur."

He really thought this was true, and Wendy, who was now in her night-gown, believed it also, and she said, to encourage Michael, "That medicine you sometimes take, father, is much nastier, isn't it?"

"Ever so much nastier," Mr. Darling said bravely, "and I would take it now as an example to you, Michael, if I hadn't lost the bottle."

He had not exactly lost it; he had climbed in the dead of night to the top of the wardrobe and hidden it there. What he did not know was that the faithful Liza had found it, and put it back on his washstand.

"I know where it is, father," Wendy cried, always glad to be of service. "I'll bring it," and she was off before he

---

Pamper ['pæmpɚ] v. 溺愛

could stop her. Immediately his spirits sank in the strangest way.

"John," he said, shuddering, "it's most beastly stuff. It's that nasty, sticky, sweet kind."

"It will soon be over, father," John said cheerily, and then Wendy rushed in with the medicine in a glass.

"I have been as quick as I could," she panted.

"You have been wonderfully quick," her father retorted, with a vindictive politeness that was quite thrown away upon her. "Michael first," he said doggedly.

"Father first," said Michael, who was of a suspicious nature. "I shall be sick, you know," Mr. Darling said threateningly.

Wendy was quite puzzled. "I thought you took it quite easily, father."

"That is not the point," he retorted. "The point is, that there is more in my glass than in Michael's spoon." His proud heart was nearly bursting.

"Father, I am waiting," said Michael coldly.

"It's all very well to say you are waiting; so am I waiting."

Wendy had a splendid idea. "Why not both take it at the same time?"

"Certainly," said Mr. Darling. "Are you ready, Michael?"

Wendy gave the words, one, two, three, and Michael took his medicine, but Mr. Darling slipped his behind his back.

There was a yell of rage from Michael, and "Oh father!" Wendy exclaimed.

It was dreadful the way all the three were looking at him, just as if they did not admire him. "Look here, all of you," he said entreatingly, as soon as Nana had gone into the bathroom, "I have just thought of a splendid joke. I shall pour my medicine into Nana's bowl, and she will drink it, thinking it is milk!"

It was the colour of milk; but the children did not have their father's sense of humour, and they looked at him reproachfully as he poured the medicine into Nana's bowl. "What fun!" he said doubtfully, and they did not dare expose him when Mrs. Darling and Nana returned.

"Nana, good dog," he said, patting her, "I have put a little milk into your bowl, Nana."

Nana wagged her tail, ran to the medicine, and began lapping it. Then she gave Mr. Darling such a look, not an angry look: she showed him the great red tear, and crept into her kennel.

 Reproachfully [rɪˈprotʃfəlɪ] adv. 責備地

Mr. Darling was frightfully ashamed of himself, but he would not give in. In a horrid silence Mrs. Darling smelt the bowl. "Oh George," she said, "it's your medicine!"

"It, was only a joke," he roared, while she comforted her boys, and Wendy hugged Nana. "Great," he said bitterly, "my wearing myself to the bone trying to be fun- ny in this house."

And still Wendy hugged Nana. "That's right," he shouted. "Coddle her! Nobody coddles me. I am only the breadwinner!"

"George," Mrs. Darling entreated him, "not so loud; the servants will hear you." Somehow they had got into the way of calling Liza the servants.

"Let them!" he answered recklessly. "Bring in the whole world. But I refuse to allow that dog to lord it in my nursery for an hour longer."

The children wept, and Nana ran to him beseechingly, but he waved her back. He felt he was a strong man again. "In vain, in vain," he cried; "the proper place for you is the yard, and there you go to be tied up this instant."

"George, George," Mrs. Darling whispered, "remember what I told you about that boy."

Beseechingly [bɪˈsitʃɪŋlɪ] adv. 懇求地

But Mr. Darling would not listen. He was determined to show everyone who was the master in the house, and so Nana went out.

In the meantime, Mrs. Darling had put the children to bed in unwonted silence and lit their night-lights. They could hear Nana barking, and John whimpered, "It is because father is chaining her up in the yard."

Wendy was wiser, "That is not Nana's unhappy bark," she said, "that is her bark when she smells danger."

Danger!

"Are you sure, Wendy?"

"Oh yes."

Mrs. Darling quivered and went to the window. It was securely fastened. She looked out, and the night was peppered with stars.

Even Michael, already half asleep, knew that she was perturbed, and he asked, "Can anything harm us, mother, after the night-lights are lit?"

"Nothing, precious," she said; "they are the eyes a mother leaves behind her to guard her children."

She went from bed to bed singing enchantments over them, and little Michael flung his arms round her. "Mother," he cried, "I'm glad of you." They were the last words she was to hear from him for a long time.

No. 27 was only a few yards distant, but there had been a slight fall of snow, and Mr. and Mrs. Darling picked their way over it deftly not to soil their shoes. They were already the only persons in the street, and all the stars were watching them. So as soon as the door of 27 closed on, there was a commotion in the firmament, and the smallest of all the stars in the Milky Way screamed out:

"Now, Peter!"

Commotion [kəˈmoʃən] n. 喧鬧

CHAPTER 3

COME AWAY, COME AWAY!

For a moment after Mr. and Mrs. Darling left the house, the night-lights by the beds of the three children continued to burn clearly. Wendy's light blinked and gave such a yawn that the other two yawned also, and before they could close their mouths all the three went out.

There was another light in the room now, a thousand times brighter than the night-lights. It was not really a light. Inside was fairy, no bigger than your hand. It was a girl called Tinker Bell exquisitely gowned in a skeleton leaf, cut low and square, through which her figure could be seen to the best advantage. She was slightly inclined to embonpoint.

A moment after the fairy's entrance, the window was blown open by the breathing of the little stars, and Peter dropped in.

"Tink, where are you?" he called softly, She was in a jug

Yawn [jɔn] n. 呵欠
Embonpoint [ˌambam'pwaŋ] n. 豐滿的體態

for the moment, and liking it extremely; she had never been in a jug before.

"Oh, do come out of that jug, and tell me, do you know where they put my shadow?"

The loveliest tinkle as of golden bells answered him. It is the fairy language.

Tink said that the shadow was in the chest of drawers, and Peter jumped at the drawers, scattering their contents to the floor with both hands. In a moment he had recovered his shadow, and in his delight he forgot that he had shut Tinker Bell up in the drawer.

If he thought at all, he would think that he and his shadow, when brought near each other, would join like drops of water, and when they did not he was appalled. He tried to stick it on with soap from the bathroom, but that also failed. A shudder passed through Peter, and he sat on the floor and cried.

His sobs woke Wendy, and she sat up in bed.

"Boy," she said courteously, "why are you crying?"

Peter could be exceedingly polite also, having learned

---

toss [tɔs] v. 拋；投
Recovered [rɪˋkʌvɚ] v. 重新找到
Shudder [ˋʃʌdɚ] n. 戰慄；發抖

the grand manner at fairy ceremonies, and he rose and bowed to her beautifully. Wendy was much pleased, and bowed beautifully to him from the bed.

"What's your name?" he asked.

"Wendy Moira Angela Darling," she replied with some satisfaction. "What's your name?"

"Peter Pan."

She asked where he lived.

"Second to the right," said Peter, "and then straight on till morning."

"What a funny address!"

Peter had a sinking. For the first time he felt that perhaps it was a funny address.

"No, it isn't," he said.

"I mean," Wendy said nicely, remembering that she was hostess, "is that what they put on the letters?"

He wished she had not mentioned letters. "Don't get any letters," he said contemptuously.

"But your mother gets letters?"

"Don't have a mother," he said. Not only had he no

Satisfaction [ˌsætɪsˈfækʃən] n. 滿意；滿足
Mention [ˈmɛnʃən] v. 提起；說到

mother, but he had not the slightest desire to have one. He thought them very over-rated persons. Wendy, however, felt at once that she was in the presence of a tragedy.

"Oh Peter, no wonder you were crying," she said, and got out of bed and ran to him.

"I wasn't crying about mothers," he said rather indignantly. "I was crying because I can't get my shadow to stick on. Do you have any glue?"

Wendy smiled. **How exactly like a boy!**

Fortunately she knew at once what to do. "It must be sewn on," she said, just a little patronisingly. she got out her housewife , and sewed the shadow on to Peter's foot.

"I daresay it will hurt a little," she warned him.

"Oh, I shan't cry," said Peter, who was already of opinion that he had never cried in his life. And he clenched his teeth and did not cry, and soon his shadow was behaving properly, though still a little creased.

"Perhaps I should have ironed it," Wendy said thoughtfully, but Peter, boylike, was indifferent to appearances, and he was now jumping about in the wildest glee. Alas, he had already forgotten that he owed his bliss to Wendy. He thought he had attached the shadow himself.

Daresay ['dɛr,se] v. 料想

"How clever I am!" he crowed rapturously.

It is humiliating to have to confess that this conceit of Peter was one of his most fascinating qualities.

But for the moment Wendy was shocked. "You conceit," she exclaimed, with frightful sarcasm; "of course I did nothing!"

"You did a little," Peter said carelessly, and continued to dance.

"A little!" she replied with hauteur. "If I am no use I can at least withdraw," and she sprang in the most dignified way into bed and covered her face with the blankets.

To induce her to look up, he pretended to be going away, and when this failed he sat on the end of the bed and tapped her gently with his foot. "Wendy," he said, in a voice that no woman has ever yet been able to resist, "Wendy, one girl is more use than twenty boys."

"Do you really think so, Peter?"

"Yes, I do."

Wendy said she would give him a kiss if he liked, but Peter did not know what she meant, and he held out his hand expectantly.

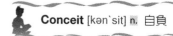
Conceit [kən`sit] n. 自負

"Surely you know what a kiss is?" she asked, aghast.

"I shall know when you give it to me," he replied stiffly, and not to hurt his feelings she gave him a thimble.

"Now," said he, "shall I give you a kiss?" and she replied with a slight primness, "If you please." She made herself rather cheap by inclining her face toward him, but he merely dropped an acorn button into her hand, so she slowly returned her face to where it had been before, and said nicely that she would wear his kiss on the chain round her neck.

When people in our set are introduced, it is customary for them to ask each other's age, and so Wendy, who always liked to do the correct thing, asked Peter how old he was.

"I don't know," he replied uneasily. He really knew nothing about it, he had merely suspicions, but he said at a venture, "Wendy, I ran away the day I was born."

"why?" Wendy asked.

"I didn't want to grow up," he said with passion. "I want always to be a little boy and to have fun. So I ran away to Kensington Gardens and lived a long long time among the fairies."

"Fairies?" Wendy breathed,wide-eyed." he told her about the beginning of fairies.

"You see, Wendy, when the first baby laughed for the

first time, its laugh broke into a thousand pieces, and they all went skipping about, and that was the beginning of fairies."

A tedious talk it was, but being a stay-at-home she liked it.

"And so," he went on good-naturedly, "there ought to be one fairy for every boy and girl."

"Ought to be? Isn't there?"

"No. You see children know such a lot now, they soon don't believe in fairies, and every time a child says, 'I don't believe in fairies,' there is a fairy somewhere that falls down dead."

Really, he thought they had now talked enough about fairies, and it struck him that Tinker Bell was keeping very quiet. "I can't think where she has gone to," he said, rising, and he called Tink by name. Wendy's heart went flutter with a sudden thrill.

"Peter," she cried, clutching him, "you don't mean to tell me that there is a fairy in this room!"

"She was here just now," he said a little impatiently. "You don't hear her, do you?" and they both listened.

"The only sound I hear," said Wendy, "is like a tinkle of

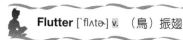

Flutter [ˈflʌtɚ] v. （鳥）振翅

bells."

The sound came from the chest of drawers, and Peter made a merry face.

"Wendy," he whispered gleefully, "I do believe I shut her up in the drawer!"

He let poor Tink out of the drawer, and she flew about the nursery screaming with fury.

Wendy was not listening to him. "Oh Peter," she cried, "if she would only stand still and let me see her!"

"They hardly ever stand still," he said, but for one moment Wendy saw the romantic figure come to rest on the cuckoo clock. "Lovely!" she cried, though Tink's face was still distorted with passion.

"Tink," said Peter amiably, "this lady says she wishes you were her fairy." Tinker Bell answered insolently.

"She is quite a common fairy," Peter explained apologetically, "she is called Tinker Bell because she mends the pots and kettles."

They were together in the armchair by this time, and Wendy plied him with more questions. He told her all about the lost boy, who had fallen out of their strollers when they were babies and never been claimed.

Apologetically [ə͵pɑlə`dʒɛtɪk!ɪ] **adv.** 道歉地

"I'm captain."

"What fun! But are there no girls on the island?"

"Oh no; girls, you know, are much too clever to fall out of their prams."

"What a nice thing to say, so you may give me a thimble." Wendy replied, blushing.

Sunddenly Wendy screamed. She felt as if someone had pulled her hair.

"That must have been Tink. I never knew her so naughty before." And indeed Tink was darting about again, using offensive language.

"She says she will do that to you, Wendy, every time I give you a thimble."

"But why?"

"Why, Tink?"

Tink replied, "You silly ass." Peter could not understand why, but Wendy understood, and she was just slightly disappointed when he admitted that he came to the nursery window not to see her but to listen to stories.

"Do you know," Peter asked, "why swallows build in the eaves of houses? It is to listen to the stories. Oh Wendy, your mother was telling you such a lovely story."

 Disappointed [ˌdɪsəˈpɔɪntɪd] **adj.** 沮喪的

"Which story was it?"

"About the prince who couldn't find the lady who wore the glass slipper."

"Peter," said Wendy excitedly, "that was Cinderella, and he found her, and they lived happily ever after."

Peter was so glad that he rose from the floor, where they had been sitting, and hurried to the window. "Where are you going?" she cried with misgiving.

"To tell the other boys."

"Don't go Peter," she entreated, "I know such lots of stories."

"Wendy, do come with me and tell the other boys."

Of course she was very pleased to be asked, but she said, "Oh dear, I can't. Think of mummy! Besides, I can't fly."

"I'll teach you."

"Oh, how lovely to fly."

"I'll teach you how to jump on the wind's back, and then away we go."

"Oo!" she exclaimed rapturously.

"Think how much the lost boys will love you," Peter continued. "you could tuck us in at night."

"And you could darn our clothes, and make pockets for us. None of us has any pockets."

How could she resist. "Of course it's awfully fascinating!" she cried. "Peter, would you teach John and Michael to fly too?"

"If you like," he said indifferently, and she ran to John and Michael and shook them. "Wake up," she cried, "Peter Pan has come and he is to teach us to fly."

John rubbed his eyes. "Then I shall get up," he said. Michael was up by this time also.

Sunddenly Peter spun around. "Shhh," he said. All was as still as salt. Then everything was right. Nana, who had been barking distressfully all the evening, was quiet now. It was her silence they had heard!

"Out with the light! Hide! Quick!" cried John, taking command for the only time throughout the whole adventure. And thus when Liza entered, holding Nana, the nursery seemed quite its old self, very dark, and you could have sworn you heard its three wicked inmates breathing angelically as they slept. They were really doing it artfully from behind the window curtains.

"There, you suspicious brute," she said, not sorry that Nana was in disgrace. "They are perfectly safe, aren't they?

Disgrace [dis'gres] n. 丟臉

Nana knew that kind of breathing, and she tried to drag herself out of Liza's clutches. But Liza was dense. "No more of it, Nana," she said sternly, pulling her out of the room.

Unfortunately Liza returned to her puddings, and Nana, seeing that no help would come from her, strained and strained at the chain until at last she broke it. In another moment she had burst into the dining-room of 27 and flung up her paws to heaven, her most expressive way of making a communication. Mr. and Mrs. Darling knew at once that something terrible was happening in their nursery, and without a good-bye to their hostess they rushed into the street.

"It's all right," John announced, emerging from his hiding-place. "I say, Peter, can you really fly?"

Instead of troubling to answer him Peter flew round the room, taking the mantelpiece on the way.

It looked delightfully easy, and they tried it first from the floor and then from the beds, but they always went down instead of up.

Of course Peter had been trifling with them, for no one can fly unless the fairy dust has been blown on him.

One of his hands was messy with it, and he blew some

 Wriggle [ˈrɪgl] v. 扭動；蠕動

on each of them, with the most superb results.

"Now just wriggle your shoulders this way," he said, "and let go."

They were all on their beds, and gallant Michael let go first. He did not quite mean to let go, but he did it, and immediately he was borne across the room.

They were not nearly so elegant as Peter, they could not help kicking a little, but their heads were bobbing against the ceiling, and there is almost nothing so delicious as that.

"I say," cried John, "why shouldn't we all go out!"

Of course it was to this that Peter had been luring them.

It was just at this moment that Mr. and Mrs. Darling hurried with Nana out of 27. They ran into the middle of the street to look up at the nursery window; and, yes, it was still shut, but the room was ablaze with light, and most heart-gripping sight of all, they could see in shadow on the curtain three little figures in night attire circling round and round, not on the floor but in the air.

Not three figures, four!

Ablaze [ə`blez] n. 閃閃發光

In a tremble they opened the street door. Mr. Darling would have rushed upstairs, but Mrs. Darling signed to him to go softly. She even tried to make her heart go softly.

They would have reached the nursery in time had it not been that the little stars were watching them. Once again the stars blew the window open, and that smallest star of all called out:

"Cave, Peter!"

Peter knew that there was not a moment to lose. "Come," he cried imperiously, and soared out at once into the night, followed by John and Michael and Wendy.

Mr. and Mrs. Darling and Nana rushed into the nursery too late.

CHAPTER4

T HE FLIGHT

"Second to the right, and straight on till morning!"

That, Peter had told Wendy, was the way to the Neverland; but even birds, carrying maps and consulting them at windy corners, could not have sighted it with these instructions. And so Michael and Wendy and John had no choice but to follow Peter, and to trust him completely.

He led them around in circles, flying past church spires and clock towers or any other tall objects on the way that took their fancy.

Sometimes it was dark and sometimes light, and now they were very cold and again too warm. His way was to pursue birds who had food in their mouths suitable for humans and snatch it from them; then the birds would follow and snatch it back; and they would all go chasing each other gaily for miles, parting at last with mutual expressions of goodwill.

 Expressions [ɪkˈsprɛʃən] n. 表達

They could now fly strongly, though they still kicked far too much.

Peter was not with them for the moment, and they felt rather lonely up there by themselves. He could go so much faster than they that he would suddenly shoot out of sight, to have some adventure in which they had no share. he would come up with mermaid scales still sticking to him, and yet not be able to say for certain what had been happening.

Peter always cames back, but sometimes he seemed barely to remember them, as if he had already moved on to his next adventure. once even Wendy had to call him by name.

"I'm Wendy," she said agitatedly.

He was very sorry. "I say, Wendy," he whispered to her, "always if you see me forgetting you, just keep on saying 'I'm Wendy,' and then I'll remember."

Of course this was rather unsatisfactory. However, to make amends he showed them how to lie out flat on a strong wind that was going their way, and this was such a pleasant change that they tried it several times and found that they could sleep thus with security.

They drew near the Neverland; for after many moons they did reach it, and, what is more, they had been going

pretty straight all the time, not perhaps so much owing to the guidance of Peter or Tink because the island was out looking for them.

Wendy and John and Michael stood on tip-toe in the air to get their first sight of the island. Strange to say, they all recognised it at once, and until fear fell upon them they hailed it, not as something long dreamt of and seen at last, but as a familiar friend to whom they were returning home for the holidays.

It was getting darker every moment, there were no night-lights or Nana to keep a child safe. The children were on their own.

They had been flying apart, but they huddled close to Peter now. They were now over the fearsome island, flying so low that sometimes a tree grazed their feet. Nothing horrid was visible in the air, yet their progress had become slow and laboured, exactly as if they were pushing their way through hostile forces. Sometimes they hung in the air until Peter had beaten on it with his fists.

"They don't want us to land," he explained. "Who are they?" Wendy whispered, shuddering.

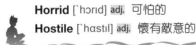

Horrid ['hɒrɪd] adj. 可怕的
Hostile ['hɒstɪl] adj. 懷有敵意的

But he could not or would not say. Tinker Bell had been asleep on his shoulder, but now he wakened her and sent her on in front.

Sometimes he poised himself in the air, listening intently, with his hand to his ear, and again he would stare down with eyes so bright that they seemed to bore two holes to earth. Having done these things, he went on again.

His courage was almost appalling. "Would you like an adventure now," he said casually to John, "or would you like to have your tea first?"

"What kind of adventure?" he asked cautiously.

"There's a pirate asleep in the pampas just beneath us," Peter told him. "If you like, we'll go down and kill him."

"Suppose," John said, a little huskily, "he were to wake up."

Peter spoke indignantly. "You don't think I would kill him while he was sleeping! I would wake him first, and then kill him. That's the way I always do."

John said "how ripping," but decided to have tea first. He asked if there were many pirates on the island just now, and Peter said he had never known so many.

"Who is captain now?"

"Hook," answered Peter, and his face became very stern as he said that hated word.

"Jas. Hook?"

Then indeed Michael began to cry, and even John could speak in gulps only, for they knew Hook's reputation.

"Of course, Hook's not quite as big as he used to be, I cut off his right hand." Peter continued, "if we meet Hook in open fight, you must leave him to me."

"I promise," John said loyally.

For the moment they were feeling less eerie, because Tink was flying with them, and in her light they could distinguish each other. Unfortunately she could not fly so slowly as they, and so she had to go round and round them in a circle in which they moved as in a halo. Wendy quite liked it, until Peter pointed out the drawback.

Tinker Bell's light might make it easier for the pirates to see them.

"Tell her to go away at once, Peter," the three cried simultaneously, but he refused.

"She thinks we have lost the way," he replied stiffly, "and she is rather frightened. You don't think I would send her away all by herself when she is frightened!"

For a moment the circle of light was broken, and something gave Peter a loving little pinch.

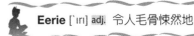

Eerie [ˈɪrɪ] adj. 令人毛骨悚然地

"Then tell her," Wendy begged, "to put out her light."

"She can't put it out. That is the only thing fairies can't do. It just goes out of itself when she falls asleep, same as the stars."

He had a happy idea. **John's hat!**

Tink agreed to travel by hat if it was carried in the hand. John carried it, though she had hoped to be carried by Peter. Presently Wendy took the hat, because John said it struck against his knee as he flew.

In the black topper the light was completely hidden, and they flew on in silence. It was the stillest silence they had ever known, broken once by a distant lapping, which Peter explained was the wild beasts drinking at the ford, and again by a rasping sound that might have been the branches of trees rubbing together, but he said it was the redskins sharpening their knives.

Even these noises ceased. To Michael the loneliness was dreadful. "If only something would make a sound!" he cried.

As if in answer to his request, the air was rent by the most tremendous crash he had ever heard. The pirates had fired Long Tom at them.

Hidden ['hɪdn] adj. 隱藏的

Thus sharply did the terrified three learn the difference between an island of make-believe and the same island come true.

When at last the heavens were steady again, John and Michael found themselves alone in the darkness. John was treading the air mechanically, and Michael without knowing how to float was floating.

"Are you shot?" John whispered tremulously. "I haven't tried yet," Michael whispered back.

Peter, however, had been carried by the wind of the shot far out to sea, while Wendy was blown upwards with no companion but Tinker Bell.

Tink was not all bad; but Fairies have to be one thing or the other, because being so small they unfortunately have room for one feeling only at a time. At present she was full of jealousy of Wendy.

Seeing a chance to rid herself of Wendy, Tink gestured for the girl to follow her. Wendy did not yet know that Tink hated her with the fierce hatred of a very woman. And so, bewildered, and now staggering in her flight, she followed Tink to her doom.

CHAPTER 5

THE ISLAND COME TRUE

Feeling that Peter was on his way back, the Neverland had again woke into life.

In his absence things are usually quiet on the island. The fairies take an hour longer in the morning, the beasts attend to their young, the Indians feed heavily for six days and nights, and when pirates and lost boys meet they merely bite their thumbs at each other.

On this evening the chief forces of the island were disposed as follows. The lost boys were out looking for Peter, the pirates were out looking for the lost boys, the Indians were out looking for the pirates, and the beasts were out looking for the Indians. They were going round and round the island, but they did not meet because all were going at the same rate.

The first to pass is Tootles, not the least brave but the most unfortunate of all that gallant band. This ill-luck had

Absence [ˈæbsns] n. 不在；缺席

given a gentle melancholy to his countenance, but instead of souring his nature had sweetened it, so that he was quite the humblest of the boys.

Next comes Nibs, the gay and debonair, followed by Slightly, who cuts whistles out of the trees and dances ecstatically to his own tunes. Slightly is the most conceited of the boys. Curly is fourth; he is a pickle, and so often has he had to deliver up his person when Peter said sternly, "Stand forth the one who did this thing," that now at the command he stands forth automatically whether he has done it or no. Last come the Twins, who cannot be described because we should be sure to be describing the wrong one.

The boys vanish in the gloom, and after a pause, but not a long pause, for things go briskly on the island, come the pirates on their track. We hear them before they are seen, and it is always the same dreadful song.

Leading their ragged group is the handsome Italian pirate Cecco, who cut his name in letters of blood on the back of the governor of the prison. Behind him is the giant, tattooed Bill Jukes. Next are Cookson and Gentleman

Melancholy [ˈmɛlənˌkɑlɪ] adj. 憂鬱的
Pickle [ˈpɪk!] n. 淘氣鬼

Starkey. Starkey is the most polite of the pirates; once an usher in school and still dainty in his ways of killing. Then come the Irish pirate, Smee, and Noodler, followed by a few more ruffians.

In the midst of them, the blackest and largest jewel in that dark setting, reclined James Hook. In person he was cadaverous and blackavized, and his hair was dressed in long curls. His eyes were of the blue of the forget-me- not, and of a profound melancholy, save when he was plunging his hook into you, at which time two red spots appeared in them and lit them up horribly. He was never more sinister than when he was most polite, which is probably the truest test of breeding; and the elegance of his diction, even when he was swearing, no less than the distinction of his demeanour, showed him one of a different caste from his crew. A man of indomitable courage, it was said of him that the only thing he shied at was the sight of his own blood, which was thick and of an unusual colour.

After the pirates come the Indians. Creeping quietly like shadows, they carry tomahawks and knives. Among them is Tiger Lily, the beautiful Indian princess, proudly erect, a

Tattooed [tæˋtu] v. 刺青

Distinction [dɪˋstɪŋkʃən] n. 區別

princess in her own right.

Behind the Indians creep the beasts- lions, tigers, bears, and the innumerable smaller savage things that flee from them.

When they have passed, comes the last figure of all, a gigantic crocodile.

The crocodile passes, but soon the boys appear again, for the procession must continue indefinitely until one of the parties stops or changes its pace. Then quickly they will be on top of each other.

The first to fall out of the moving circle was the boys. They flung themselves down on the sward, close to their underground home.

"I do wish Peter would come back, and tell us whether he has heard anything more about Cinderella." Slightly said.

They talked of Cinderella, and Tootles was confident that his mother must have been very like her.

It was only in Peter's absence that they could speak of mothers, the subject being forbidden by him as silly. The lost boys had stopped, but the pirates were still coming.

With the exception of Nibs, who has darted away to reconnoitre, they are already in their home under the

Crocodile [ˈkrɑkəˌdaɪl] **n.** 鱷魚

ground. But how have they reached it? for there is no entrance to be seen, not so much as a large stone, which if rolled away would disclose the mouth of a cave. Look closely, however, and you may note that there are here seven large trees, each with a hole in its hollow trunk as large as a boy These are the seven entrances to the home under the ground.

As the pirates advanced, the quick eye of Starkey sighted Nibs disappearing through the wood, and at once his pistol flashed out. But an iron claw gripped his shoulder.

"Captain, let go!" he cried, writhing.

"Put back that pistol first," Hook said threateningly.

"It was one of those boys you hate. I could have shot him dead."

"Not now, Smee," Hook said darkly. "He is only one, and I want to mischief all the seven. Scatter and look for them."

The pirates disappeared among the trees, and in a moment their captain and Smee were alone. Hook heaved a heavy sigh.

"Most of all," Hook was saying passionately, "I want their captain, Peter Pan. 'Twas he cut off my arm." He

Scatter [ˈskætə-] v. 亂扔

brandished the hook threateningly. "I've waited long to shake his hand with this. Oh, I'll tear him!"

"Peter flung my arm," he said, wincing, "to a crocodile that happened to be passing by."

"I have often," said Smee, "noticed your strange dread of crocodiles."

"Not of crocodiles," Hook corrected him, "but of that one crocodile." He lowered his voice. "It liked my arm so much, Smee, that it has followed me ever since, from sea to sea and from land to land, licking its lips for the rest of me."

He sat down on a large mushroom, and now there was a quiver in his voice. "Smee," he said huskily, "that crocodile would have had me before this, but by a lucky chance it swallowed a clock which goes tick tick inside it, and so before it can reach me I hear the tick and bolt." He laughed, but in a hollow way.

"Some day," said Smee, "the clock will run down, and then he'll get you." Hook wetted his dry lips. "Ay," he said, "that's the fear that haunts me."

Since sitting down he had felt curiously warm. "Smee," he said, "this seat is hot."

They examined the mushroom, which was of a size and solidity unknown on the mainland; they tried to pull it up,

and it came away at once in their hands, for it had no root. Stranger still, smoke began at once to ascend. The pirates looked at each other. "A chimney!" they both exclaimed.

Not only smoke came out of it. There came also children's voices, for so safe did the boys feel in their hiding-place that they were gaily chattering. The pirates listened grimly, and then replaced the mushroom. They looked around them and noted the holes in the seven trees.

"Did you hear them say Peter Pan's from home?" Smee whispered, fidgeting with Johnny Corkscrew.

Hook nodded. He stood for a long time lost in thought, and at last a curdling smile lit up his swarthy face.

"To return to the ship," Hook said. "and cook a large rich cake of a jolly thickness with green sugar on it. We will leave the cake on the shore of the Mermaids' Lagoon. These boys are always swimming about there, playing with the mermaids. They will find the cake and they will gobble it up, because, having no mother, they don't know how dangerous 'tis to eat rich damp cake." He burst into laughter, not hollow laughter now, but honest laughter.

They began the verse, but they never finished it, for another sound broke in and stilled them.

Curiously [ˈkjuriəsli] adv. 好奇地

Tick tick tick tick!

Hook stood shuddering, one foot in the air.

"The crocodile!" he gasped, and bounded away, followed by his bo'sun.

Once more the boys emerged into the open. Suddenly Nibs saw something in the sky.

"I have seen a wonderfuller thing," he cried, as they gathered round him eagerly. "A great white bird. It is flying this way."

"What kind of a bird, do you think?"

"I don't know," Nibs said, awestruck, "but it looks so weary, and as it flies it moans, 'Poor Wendy.'"

Wendy was now almost overhead, and they could hear her plaintive cry. But more distinct came the shrill voice of Tinker Bell. The jealous fairy had now cast off all disguise of friendship, and was darting at her victim from every direction, pinching savagely each time she touched.

"Hullo, Tink," cried the wondering boys.

Tink's reply rang out: "Peter wants you to shoot the Wendy."

Damp [dæmp] adj. 消沉的
Jealous [ˈdʒɛləs] adj. 忌妒的

"Quick, Tootles, quick," she screamed. "Peter will be so pleased."

Tootles excitedly fitted the arrow to his bow. "Out of the way, Tink," he shouted, and then he fired, and Wendy fluttered to the ground with an arrow in her breast.

CHAPTER 6

THE LITTLE HOUSE

"I have shot the Wendy." Tootles cried proudly, "Peter will be so proud of me."

They had crowded round Wendy, and as they looked a terrible silence fell upon the wood. If Wendy's heart had been beating they would all have heard it.

Slightly was the first to speak. "This is no bird," he said in a scared voice. "I think it must be a lady."

"Now I see," Curly said; "Peter was bringing her to us." He threw himself sorrowfully on the ground.

"I did it," he said, reflecting, and He moved slowly away.

"Don't go," they called in pity.

"I must," he answered, shaking; "I am so afraid of Peter."

It was at this tragic moment that they heard a sound which made the heart of every one of them rise to his mouth. They heard Peter crow.

"Greeting, boys," he cried, and mechanically they saluted, and then again was silence.

He frowned.

They opened their mouths, but the cheers would not come. He overlooked it in his haste to tell the glorious tidings.

"Great news, boys," he cried, "I've brought you back a mother! I think she was flying this way."

Tootles said, "Back, twins, let Peter see."

So they all stood back, and let him see, and after he had looked for a little time he did not know what to do next.

"Whose arrow?" he demanded sternly.

"Mine, Peter," said Tootles on his knees.

"Oh, dastard hand," Peter said, and he raised the arrow to use it as a dagger.

Twice did Peter raise the arrow, and twice did his hand fall. "I cannot strike," he said with awe, "there is something stays my hand."

All looked at him in wonder, save Nibs, who fortunately looked at Wendy. "It is she," he cried, "the Wendy lady, see, her arm!"

"She lives," Peter said briefly.

Slightly cried instantly, "The Wendy lady lives."

Then Peter knelt beside her and found his button.

Dastard ['dæstə-d] adj. 卑劣的

Wendy had put it on a chain that she wore round her neck.

"See," he said, "the arrow struck against this. It is the kiss I gave her. It has saved her life."

"I remember kisses," Slightly interposed quickly, "let me see it. Ay, that's a kiss."

Peter did not hear him. He was begging Wendy to get better quickly, so that he could show her the mermaids. Of course she could not answer yet, being still in a frightful faint; but from overhead came a wailing note.

"Listen to Tink," said Curly, "she is crying because the Wendy lives."

Then they had to tell Peter of Tink's crime, and almost never had they seen him look so stern.

"Listen, Tinker Bell," he cried, "I am your friend no more. Begone from me forever."

She flew on to his shoulder and pleaded, but he brushed her off. Not until Wendy again raised her arm did he relent sufficiently to say, "Well, not forever, but for a whole week."

Do you think Tinker Bell was grateful to Wendy for raising her arm? Oh dear no, never wanted to pinch her so much.

But what to do with Wendy in her present delicate state of health?

"I have an idea," Peter said. "Let us build a little house

round her."

They were all delighted. In a moment they were as busy as tailors the night before a wedding. They scurried this way and that, down for bedding, up for firewood, and while they were at it, who should appear but John and Michael. As they dragged along the ground they fell asleep standing, stopped, woke up, moved another step and slept again.

You may be sure they were very relieved to find Peter.

"Hullo, Peter," they said.

"Hullo," replied Peter amicably, though he had quite forgotten them. He was very busy at the moment measuring Wendy with his feet to see how large a house she would need. Of course he meant to leave room for chairs and a table. John and Michael watched him.

"Curly," said Peter in his most captainy voice, "see that these boys help in the building of the house."

"Ay, ay, sir."

"Build a house?" exclaimed John.

"For the Wendy," said Curly.

"For Wendy?" John said, aghast. "Why, she is only a girl!"

"That," explained Curly, "is why we are her servants."

scurry [ˈskɜ·ɪ] v. 急匆匆地跑

"You? Wendy's servants!"

"Yes," said Peter, "and you also. Away with them."

The astounded brothers were dragged away to hack and hew and carry. "Chairs and a fender first," Peter ordered. "Then we shall build the house round them."

In the meantime the wood had been alive with the sound of axes; almost everything needed for a cosy dwelling already lay at Wendy's feet.

The house was quite beautiful, and no doubt Wendy was very cosy within, though, of course, they could no longer see her. Peter strode up and down, ordering finishing touches. Nothing escaped his eagle eye. Just when it seemed absolutely finished,

"There's no knocker on the door," he said.

They were very ashamed, but Tootles gave the sole of his shoe, and it made an excellent knocker.

Absolutely finished now, they thought.

"All look your best," Peter warned them; "first impressions are awfully important."

He knocked politely, and now the wood was as still as

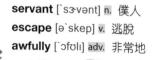

servant [ˈsɝvənt] n. 僕人

escape [əˈskep] v. 逃脫

awfully [ˈɔfʊlɪ] adv. 非常地

the children, not a sound to be heard except from Tinker Bell, who was watching from a branch and openly sneering.

The door opened and a lady came out. It was Wendy. They all whipped off their hats.

She looked properly surprised, and this was just how they had hoped she would look.

"Where am I?" she said.

Of course Slightly was the first to get his word in. "Wendy lady," he said rapidly, "for you we built this house."

"Lovely, darling house," Wendy said, and they were the very words they had hoped she would say.

"And we are your children," cried the twins.

Then all went on their knees, and holding out their arms cried, "O Wendy lady, be our mother."

"Ought I?" Wendy said, all shining. "Of course it's frightfully fascinating, but you see I'm only a little girl. I have no real experience."

"That doesn't matter," said Peter, as if he were the only person present who knew all about it, though he was really the one who knew least. "What we need is just a nice motherly person."

"Oh dear!" Wendy said, "you see I feel that is exactly

---

fascinating ['fæsn,etɪŋ] adj. 迷人的

what I am."

"It is, it is," they all cried; "we saw it at once."

"Very well," she said, "I will do my best. Come inside at once, you naughty children; I am sure your feet are damp. And before I put you to bed I have just time to finish the story of Cinderella."

CHAPTER 7

THE HOME UNDER THE GROUND

One of the first things Peter did next day was to measure Wendy and John and Michael for hollow trees. Once you fitted, you drew in your breath at the top, and down you went at exactly the right speed, while to ascend you drew in and let out alternately, and so wriggled up.

But you simply must fit, and Peter measures you for your tree as carefully as for a suit of clothes: the only difference being that the clothes are made to fit you, while you have to be made to fit the tree. Once you fit, great care must be taken to go on fitting, and this, as Wendy was to discover to her delight, keeps a whole family in perfect condition.

Wendy and Michael fitted their trees at the first try, but John had to be altered a little.

measure [ˈmɛʒə] v. 測量；計量
Ascend [əˈsɛnd] v. 上升
alternately [ˈɔltə·nɪtlɪ] adv. 交替地；輪流地

After a few days' practice they could go up and down as gaily as buckets in a well. And how ardently they grew to love their home under the ground; especially Wendy! The cave was one large, cozy room with a floor made of dirt. The boys used mushrooms as chairs and a sawed-off tree trunk as a table.

There was an enormous fireplace which was in almost any part of the room where you cared to light it, and across this Wendy stretched strings, made of fibre, from which she suspended her washing. The bed was tilted against the wall by day, and let down at 6:30, when it filled nearly half the room; and all the boys slept in it, except Michael, lying like sardines in a tin. There was a strict rule against turning round until one gave the signal, when all turned at once. Michael should have used it also, but Wendy would have a baby, and he was the littlest, and the short and the long of it is that he was hung up in a basket.

It was rough and simple, and not unlike what baby bears would have made of an underground house in the same circumstances. But there was one recess in the wall, no

Stretch [strɛtʃ] v. 拉長
circumstance [ˈsɝkəmˌstæns] n. 情況

larger than a birdcage, which was the private apartment of Tinker Bell. It could be shut off from the rest of the home by a tiny curtain, which Tink, who was most fastidious, always kept drawn when dressing or undressing. No woman, however large, could have had a more exquisite boudoir.

It was all especially entrancing to Wendy, because those rampagious boys of hers gave her so much to do. Really there were whole weeks when, except perhaps with a stocking in the evening, she was never above ground. The cooking.

Wendy's favourite time for sewing and darning was after they had all gone to bed. Then, as she expressed it, she had a breathing time for herself; and she occupied it in making new things for them, and putting double pieces on the knees, for they were all most frightfully hard on their knees.

Wendy did not really worry about her father and mother, she was absolutely confident that they would always keep the window open for her to fly back by, and this gave her complete ease of mind. What did disturb her

---

Private [ˈpraɪvɪt] adj. 私人的
Darning [ˈdɑrnɪŋ] n. 織補
Disturb [dɪsˈtɜb] v. 妨礙

at times was that John remembered his parents vaguely only, as people he had once known, while Michael was quite willing to believe that she was really his mother. To fix this, Wendy set up a little school, with their old life as the subject instead of spelling or math. she tried to fix the old life in their minds by setting them examination papers on it, as like as possible to the ones she used to do at school. The other boys thought this awfully interesting, and insisted on joining, and they made slates for themselves, and sat round the table, writing and thinking hard about the questions she had written on another slate and passed round.

The other boys wanted to go to school, too, so she let them sit in. They were the most ordinary questions- "What was the colour of Mother's eyes? Which was taller, Father or Mother? Was Mother blonde or brunette? Answer all three questions if possible."

Peter did not compete. For one thing he despised all mothers except Wendy, and for another he was the only boy on the island who could neither write nor spell; not the smallest word. He was above all that sort of thing.

---

vaguely [ˈveglɪ] adv. 茫然地

ordinary [ˈɔrdnˌɛrɪ] adj. 通常的，平常的

Peter often went out alone, and when he came back you were never absolutely certain whether he had had an adventure or not. Sometimes he came home with his head bandaged, and then Wendy cooed over him and bathed it in lukewarm water, while he told a dazzling tale.

Should we take the brush with the Indians at Slightly Gulch? It was a sanguinary affair, and especially interesting as showing one of Peter's peculiarities, which was that in the middle of a fight he would suddenly change sides. At the Gulch, when victory was still in the balance, sometimes leaning this way and sometimes that, he called out, "I'm redskin today; what are you, Tootles?" And Tootles answered, "Redskin; what are you, Nibs?" and Nibs said, "Redskin; what are you, Twin?" and so on; and they were all redskin; and of course this would have ended the fight had not the real Indians, fascinated by Peter's methods, agreed to be lost boys for that once, and so at it they all went again, more fiercely than ever.

Sanguinary [ˈsæŋgwɪˌnɛrɪ] adj. 流血的
Fascinated [ˈfæsnˌetɪd] adj. 入迷的

Or we could tell of that cake the pirates cooked so that the boys might eat it and perish; and how they placed it in one cunning spot after another; but always Wendy snatched it from the hands of her children, so that in time it lost its succulence, and became as hard as stone, and was used as a missile, and Hook fell over it in the dark.

Which of these adventures shall we choose? The best way will be to toss for it.

I have tossed, and the lagoon has won.

CHAPTER 8

THE MERMAID'S LAGOON

The children often spent long summer days on this lagoon, swimming or floating most of the time, playing the mermaid games in the water, and so forth. You must not think from this that the mermaids were on friendly terms with them: on the contrary.

The most haunting time at which to see them is at the turn of the moon, when they utter strange wailing cries; but the lagoon is dangerous for mortals. Wendy knew this, and made sure that she always gathered her children and left before dark On this day.

It must also have been rather pretty to see the children resting on a rock for half an hour after their midday meal. Wendy insisted on their doing this, and it had to be a real rest even though the meal was make-believe. So they lay there in the sun, and their bodies glistened in it, while she sat beside them and looked important.

While she stitched a change came to the lagoon. Little shivers ran over it, and the sun went away and shadows

stole across the water, turning it cold. Wendy could no longer see to thread her needle, and when she looked up. It was not night that had come. It was something worse.

Of course she should have roused the children at once; not merely because of the unknown that was stalking toward them, but because it was no longer good for them to sleep on a rock grown chilly. But she was a young mother and she did not know this; she thought you simply must stick to your rule about half an hour after the midday meal.

It was well for those boys then that there was one among them who could sniff danger even in his sleep. Peter sprang erect, as wide awake at once as a dog, and with one warning cry he roused the others.

"Pirates!" he cried.

"Dive!"

There was a gleam of legs, and instantly the lagoon seemed deserted. Marooners' Rock stood alone in the forbidding waters, as if it were itself marooned.

The boat drew nearer. It was the pirate dinghy, with three figures in her, Smee and Starkey, and the third a captive, no other than Tiger Lily. Her hands and ankles were

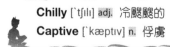

Chilly [ˈtʃɪlɪ] adj. 冷颼颼的
Captive [ˈkæptɪv] n. 俘虜

tied, and she knew what was to be her fate. Yet her face was impassive; she was the daughter of a chief, she must die as a chief's daughter, it is enough.

They had caught her boarding the pirate ship with a knife in her mouth. No watch was kept on the ship, it being Hook's boast that the wind of his name guarded the ship for a mile around. Now her fate would help to guard it also. One more wall would go the round in that wind by night.

It was the work of one brutal moment to land the beautiful girl on the rock; she was too proud to offer a vain resistance.

Quite near the rock, but out of sight, two heads were bobbing up and down, Peter's and Wendy's. Wendy was crying, for it was the first tragedy she had seen. Peter had seen many tragedies, but he had forgotten them all. He was less sorry than Wendy for Tiger Lily: it was two against one that angered him, and he meant to save her.

There was almost nothing he could not do, and he now imitated the voice of Hook.

"Set her free."

"Free!"

"Yes, cut her bonds and let her go." "But, captain-"

"At once, do you hear," cried Peter, "or I'll plunge my hook in you." "This is queer!" Smee gasped.

"Ay, ay," Smee said, and he cut Tiger Lily's cords. At once like an eel she slid between Starkey's legs into the water.

Of course Wendy was very elated over Peter's cleverness; but she knew that he would be elated also and very likely crow and thus betray himself, so at once her hand went out to cover his mouth. But it was stayed even in the act, for "Boat ahoy!" rang over the lagoon in Hook's voice, but this time it was not Peter who had spoken.

"Boat ahoy!" again came the voice.

Now Wendy understood. The real Hook was also in the water.

He was swimming to the boat, and as his men showed a light to guide him he had soon reached them. In the light of the lantern Wendy saw his hook grip the boat's side; she saw his evil swarthy face as he rose dripping from the water, and, quaking, she would have liked to swim away, but Peter would not budge.

He signed to her to listen.

The two pirates were very curious to know what had brought their captain to them, but he sat with his head on his hook in a position of profound melancholy.

 Dripping [ˈdrɪpɪŋ] adj. 濕淋淋的

"What's up, captain?"

Then at last he spoke passionately.

"The game's up," he cried, "those boys have found a mother." Affrighted though she was, Wendy swelled with pride.

"O evil day!" cried Starkey.

"What's a mother?" asked the ignorant Smee.

Just then, the nest belonging to the Never bird floated by, with the mother bird still sitting on it.

"See," said Hook in answer to Smee's question, "that is a mother. What a lesson! The nest must have fallen into the water, but would the mother desert her eggs? No."

Smee, much impressed, gazed at the bird as the nest was borne past, but the more suspicious Starkey said, "If she is a mother, perhaps she is hanging about here to help Peter."

Hook winced. "Ay," he said, "that is the fear that haunts me." He was roused from this dejection by Smee's eager voice.

"Captain," said Smee, "could we not kidnap these boys' mother and make her our mother?"

"It is a princely scheme," cried Hook, and at once it took practical shape in his great brain. "We will seize the

Kidnap ['kɪdnæp] v. 綁架；劫持

children and carry them to the boat: the boys we will make walk the plank, and Wendy shall be our mother."

"Wait, Where is the redskin?" he demanded abruptly.

He had a playful humour at moments, and they thought this was one of the moments.

"That is all right, captain," Smee answered complacently; "we let her go." "Let her go!" cried Hook.

"'Twas your own orders," the bo'sun faltered.

"You called over the water to us to let her go," said Starkey.

"Brimstone and gall," thundered Hook, "what cozening is here!" His face had gone black with rage, but he saw that they believed their words, and he was startled. "Lads," he said, shaking a little, "I gave no such order."

"It is passing queer," Smee said, and they all fidgeted uncomfortably. Hook raised his voice, but there was a quiver in it.

"Spirit that haunts this dark lagoon tonight," he cried, "dost hear me?"

Of course Peter should have kept quiet, but of course he did not. He immediately answered in Hook's voice:

"Odds, bobs, hammer and tongs, I hear you."

"Who are you, stranger, speak?" Hook demanded.

"I am James Hook," replied the voice, "captain of the Jolly Roger"

"You are not; you are not," Hook cried hoarsely.

"Brimstone and gall," the voice retorted, "say that again, and I'll cast anchor in you."

Hook tried a more ingratiating manner. "If you are Hook," he said almost humbly, "come tell me, who am I?"

"A codfish," replied the voice, "only a codfish."

"A codfish!" Hook echoed blankly, and it was then, but not till then, that his proud spirit broke. He saw his men draw back from him.

"Have we been captained all this time by a codfish!" they muttered. "It is lowering to our pride."

They were his dogs snapping at him, but, tragic figure though he had become, he scarcely heeded them. Against such fearful evidence it was not their belief in him that he needed, it was his own. He felt his ego slipping from him. "Don't desert me," he whispered hoarsely to it.

In his dark nature there was a touch of the feminine, as in all the greatest pirates, and it sometimes gave him intuitions. Suddenly he tried the guessing game.

"Hook," he called, "have you another voice?"

Hoarsely [ˈhɔrslɪ] adv. 嘶啞地

Now Peter could never resist a game, and he answered blithely in his own voice, "I have."

"And another name?"

"Ay, ay."

"Are you an animal, vegetable, or mineral?" "No."

"Man?"

"No!" This answer rang out scornfully. "Boy?"

"Yes." "Ordinary boy?" "No!"

"Wonderful boy?"

To Wendy's pain the answer that rang out this time was "Yes."

Hook was completely puzzled.

"Can't guess, can't guess!" crowed Peter. "Do you give it up?"

"Yes, yes," they answered eagerly. "Well, then," he cried, "I am Peter Pan!"

Pan!

In a moment Hook was himself again, and Smee and Starkey were his faithful henchmen.

"Now we have him," Hook shouted. "Into the water, Smee. Starkey, mind the boat. Take him dead or alive!"

Blithely [ˈblaɪðlɪ] adv. 快活地

faithful [ˈfeθfəl] adj. 忠誠的

He leaped as he spoke, and simultaneously came the gay voice of Peter. "Are you ready, boys?"

"Ay, ay" from various parts of the lagoon. "Then lam into the pirates."

The fight was short and sharp. Swords flew in the water and air, followed by many wheezes and whoops and wails as the two pirates and the lost boys clashed.

Hook and Peter had their own private battle to fight.

Strangely, it was not in the water that they met. Hook rose to the rock to breathe, and at the same moment Peter scaled it on the opposite side. The rock was slippery as a ball, and they had to crawl rather than climb.

Peter had no sinking, he had one feeling only, gladness; and he gnashed his pretty teeth with joy. Quick as thought he snatched a knife from Hook's belt and was about to drive it home, when he saw that he was higher up the rock than his foe. It would not have been fighting fair. He gave the pirate a hand to help him up.

It was then that Hook bit him.

Not the pain of this but its unfairness was what dazed Peter. It made him quite helpless. He could only stare, horrified. Every child is affected thus the first time he is treated unfairly.

Hook clawed Peter twice with his hook, and might have finished him off had he not just then heard a ticking.

A few minutes afterwards the other boys saw Hook in the water striking wildly for the ship; no elation on his pestilent face now, only white fear, for the crocodile was in dogged pursuit of him.

On ordinary occasions the boys would have swum alongside cheering; but now they were uneasy, for they had lost both Peter and Wendy, and were scouring the lagoon for them, calling them by name. They found the dinghy and went home in it, shouting "Peter, Wendy" as they went, but no answer came save mocking laughter from the mermaids. "They must be swimming back or flying," the boys concluded. They were not very anxious, they had such faith in Peter.

When their voices died away there came cold silence over the lagoon, and then a feeble cry.

"Help, help!"

Two small figures were beating against the rock; the girl had fainted and lay on the boy's arm. With a last effort Peter pulled her up the rock and then lay down beside her.

Faint [feint] adj. 頭暈的

Even as he also fainted he saw that the water was rising. He knew that they would soon be drowned, but he could do no more.

As they lay side by side a mermaid caught Wendy by the feet, and began pulling her softly into the water. Peter, feeling her slip from him, woke with a start, and was just in time to draw her back.

"We are on the rock, Wendy," he said, "but it is growing smaller. Soon the water will be over it."

"We must go," she said, almost brightly. "Yes," he answered faintly.

"Shall we swim or fly, Peter?" He had to tell her.

"Do you think you could swim or fly as far as the island, Wendy, without my help?"

She had to admit that she was too tired. He moaned.

"What is it?" she asked, anxious about him at once.

"I can't help you, Wendy. Hook wounded me. I can neither fly nor swim."

"Do you mean we shall both be drowned?"

They put their hands over their eyes to shut out the sight. They thought they would soon be no more. As they sat thus something brushed against Peter as light as a kiss, and stayed there, as if saying timidly, "Can I be of any use?"

It was the tail of a kite, which Michael had made some days before. It had torn itself out of his hand and floated away.

"Michael's kite," Peter said without interest, but next moment he had seized the tail, and was pulling the kite toward him.

"It lifted Michael off the ground," he cried; "why should it not carry you?" "Both of us!"

"It can't lift two; Michael and Curly tried."

"Let us draw lots," Wendy said bravely.

"And you a lady; never." Already he had tied the tail round her. She clung to him; she refused to go without him; but with a "Good-bye, Wendy," he pushed her from the rock; and in a few minutes she was borne out of his sight. Peter was alone on the lagoon.

The rock was very small now; soon it would be submerged. Peter was not quite like other boys; but he was afraid at last. But soon his fear changed to excitement. Next moment he was standing erect on the rock again, with that smile on his face and a drum beating within him. It was saying, "To die will be an awfully big adventure."

CHAPTER 9

THE NEVER BIRD

The last sounds Peter heard the moment he was quite alone were the mermaids retiring one by one to their bedchambers under the sea.

Steadily the waters rose till they were nibbling at his feet; and to pass the time until they made their final gulp, he watched the only thing moving on the lagoon. He thought it was a piece of floating paper, perhaps part of the kite, and wondered idly how long it would take to drift ashore.

It was not really a piece of paper; it was the Never bird, making desperate efforts to reach Peter on her nest. By working her wings, in a way she had learned since the nest fell into the water, she was able to some extent to guide her strange craft, but by the time Peter recognised her she was very exhausted. She had come to save him, to give him her nest, though there were eggs in it.

Floating [ˈfloʊtɪŋ] adj. 漂浮的
Desperate [ˈdɛspərɪt] adj. 情急拚命的
Exhausted [ɪgˈzɔstɪd] adj. 精疲力竭的

She called out to him what she had come for, and he called out to her what was she doing there; but of course neither of them understood the other's language.

"I WANT YOU TO GET INTO THE NEST" the bird called, speaking as slowly and distinctly as possible, "AND THEN YOU CAN DRIFT ASHORE"

"What are you quacking about?" Peter answered.

"I want you..." the bird said, and repeated it all over. Then Peter tried slow and distinct.

"What are you quacking about?" and so on.

The Never bird became irritated; they have very short tempers.

"You dunderheaded little jay," she screamed, "why don't you do as I tell you?"

Peter felt that she was calling him names, and at a venture he retorted hotly: "So are you!"

Then rather curiously they both snapped out the same remark. "Shut up!"

"Shut up!"

Nevertheless the bird was determined to save him if she could, and by one last mighty effort she propelled the nest

Snap [snæp] v. 厲聲說

against the rock. Then up she flew; deserting her eggs, so as to make her meaning clear.

Then at last he understood, and clutched the nest and waved his thanks to the bird as she fluttered overhead.

There were two large white eggs, and Peter lifted them up and reflected. The bird covered her face with her wings, so as not to see the last of them; but she could not help peeping between the feathers.

On the rock next to Peter was a waterproof hat, broad and wide, which Starkey had left behind. Peter put the eggs into this hat and set it on the lagoon. It floated beautifully.

The Never bird saw at once what he was up to, and screamed her admiration of him; and, alas, Peter crowed his agreement with her. Then he got into the nest. At the same moment the bird fluttered down upon the hat and once more sat snugly on her eggs. She drifted in one direction, and he was borne off in another, both cheering.

Of course when Peter landed he beached his barque in a place where the bird would easily find it; but the hat was such a great success that she abandoned the nest.

Great were the rejoicings when Peter reached the

 Abandoned [əˋbændənd] adj. 被遺棄的

home under the ground almost as soon as Wendy, who had been carried hither and thither by the kite. Every boy had adventures to tell; but perhaps the biggest adventure of all was that they were several hours late for bed. This so inflated them that they did various dodgy things to get staying up still longer, such as demanding bandages; but Wendy, though glorying in having them all home again safe and sound, was scandalised by the lateness of the hour, and cried, "To bed, to bed," in a voice that had to be obeyed.

One important result of the brush on the lagoon was that it made the Indians their friends. Peter had saved Tiger Lily from a dreadful fate, and now she and her braves would do anything for him. All night they stayed alert, keeping watch over the home under the ground and awaiting the big attack by the pirates which obviously could not be much longer delayed.

Bandage [ˋbændɪdʒ] n. 繃帶
Result [rɪˋzʌlt] n. 結果；效果

CHAPTER 10

WENDY'S STORY

"Listen," said Wendy, settling down to her story, with Michael at her feet and seven boys in the bed. "There was once a gentleman-"

"I had rather he had been a lady," Curly said.

"Quiet," their mother admonished them. "There was a lady also, and-"

"Oh mummy," cried the first twin, "you mean that there is a lady also, don't you? She is not dead, is she?"

"Little less noise there," Peter called out, determined that she should have fair play, however beastly a story it might be in his opinion.

"They were married, you know," explained Wendy, "and what do you think they had?"

"White rats!" cried Nibs, inspired. "No."

"It's awfully puzzling," said Tootles, who knew the story by heart. "Quiet, Tootles. They had three descendants."

"What is descendants?"

 Descendant [dɪˈsɛndənt] n. 子孫；後裔

"Well, you are one, Twin."

"Oh dear, oh dear," sighed Wendy. "Now these three children had a faithful nurse called Nana; but Mr. Darling was angry with her and chained her up in the yard, and so all the children flew away."

"It's an awfully good story," said Nibs.

"They flew away," Wendy continued, "to the Neverland, where the lost children are."

"I just thought they did," Curly broke in excitedly. "I don't know how it is, but I just thought they did!"

"Oh Wendy," cried Tootles, "was one of the lost children called Tootles?"

"Yes, he was."

"I am in a story, Hurrah, I am in a story, Nibs."

"Hush. Now I want you to consider the feelings of the unhappy parents with all their children flown away."

"Oo!" they all moaned, though they were not really considering the feelings of the unhappy parents one jot.

"I don't see how it can have a happy ending," said the second twin.

"If you knew how great a mother's love is," Wendy told them triumphantly, "you would have no fear." She had now

Consider [kən'sidə] v. 細想

come to the part that Peter hated.

"You see," Wendy said complacently, "our heroine knew that the mother would always leave the window open for her children to fly back by; so they stayed away for years and had a lovely time."

"Did they ever go back?"

"Let us now," said Wendy, bracing herself up for her finest effort, "take a peep into the future", and they all gave themselves the twist that makes peeps into the future easier.

"See, dear brothers," says Wendy, pointing upwards, "there is the window still standing open. Ah, now we are rewarded for our sublime faith in a mother's love. So up they flew to their mummy and daddy, and pen cannot describe the happy scene, over which we draw a veil."

From Peter's corner came a hollow groan.

"What is it, Peter?" she cried, running to him, thinking he was ill.

"It isn't that kind of pain," Peter replied darkly.

"Then what kind is it?"

"Wendy, you are wrong about mothers."

They all gathered round him in affright, so alarming was his agitation; and with a fine candour he told them what he

Sublime [səˋblaɪm] adj. 偉大的

had concealed so far.

"Long ago," he said, "I thought like you that my mother would always keep the window open for me, so I stayed away for moons, and moons and moons, and then flew back; but the window was barred, for mother had forgotten all about me, and there was another little boy sleeping in my bed."

"Are you sure mothers are like that?"

"Yes."

So this was the truth about mothers. The toads!

Still it is best to be careful; and no one knows so quickly as a child when he should give in. "Wendy, let us go home," cried John and Michael together.

"Yes," she said, clutching them.

"Not tonight?" asked the lost boys bewilderedly. They knew that one can get on quite well without a mother, and that it is only the mothers who think you can't.

"At once," Wendy replied resolutely, for the horrible thought had come to her: "Perhaps mother is in half mourning by this time."

This dread made her forgetful of what must be Peter's

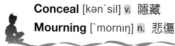

Conceal [kən`sil] v. 隱藏

Mourning [`mornɪŋ] n. 悲傷

feelings, and she said to him rather sharply, "Peter, will you make the necessary arrangements?"

"If you wish," he replied, as coolly as if she had asked him to pass the nuts.

Not so much as a farewell between them! If she did not mind the parting, he was going to show her, that neither did he.

"Wendy," he said, striding up and down, "I have asked the Indians to guide you through the wood, as flying tires you so."

"Thank you, Peter."

"Then," he continued, in the short sharp voice of one accustomed to be obeyed, "Tinker Bell will take you across the sea. Wake her, Nibs."

In the meantime the boys were gazing very forlornly at Wendy, now equipped with John and Michael for the journey. By this time they were dejected.

"Dear ones," she said, "if you will all come with me I feel almost sure I can get my father and mother to adopt you."

The invitation was meant specially for Peter, but each

Forlornly [fə`lɔrnlɪ] adv. 可憐兮兮地

of the boys was thinking exclusively of himself, and at once they jumped with joy.

"Peter, can we go?" they all cried imploringly.

"All right," Peter replied with a bitter smile, and immediately they rushed to get their things.

"And now, Peter," Wendy said, thinking she had put everything right, "I am going to give you your medicine before you go." She loved to give them medicine, and undoubtedly gave them too much. Of course it was only water, but it was out of a bottle, and she always shook the bottle and counted the drops, which gave it a certain medicinal quality. On this occasion, however, she did not give Peter his draught, for just as she had prepared it, she saw a look on his face that made her heart sink.

"Get your things, Peter," she cried, shaking.

"No," he answered, pretending indifference, "I am not going with you, Wendy."

And so the others had to be told. "Peter isn't coming."

Peter not coming! They gazed blankly at him, their sticks over their backs, and on each stick a bundle. Their first thought was that if Peter was not going he had

Certain [ˈsɝtən] adj. 確信的；可靠的
Blankly [ˈblæŋklɪ] adv. 茫然地

probably changed his mind about letting them go.

"Now then," cried Peter, "no fuss, no blubbering. Good-bye, Wendy".

That seemed to be everything, and an awkward pause followed. Peter, however, was not the kind that breaks down before people. "Are you ready, Tinker Bell?" he called out.

"Ay! ay!"

"Then lead the way."

Tink darted up the nearest tree; but no one followed her, for it was at this moment that the pirates made their dreadful attack upon the Indians. Above, where all had been so still, the air was rent with shrieks and the clash of steel. Below, there was dead silence. Mouths opened and remained open.

CHAPTER 11

THE CHILDREN ARE CARRIED OFF

The pirate attack had been a complete surprise: a sure proof that the despicable Hook had conducted it improperly, for to surprise Indians fairly is beyond the wit of the white man.

Through the long black night the savage scouts wriggle,snake-like, among the grass without stirring a blade. The brushwood closes behind them as silently as sand into which a mole has dived. Not a sound is to be heard, save when they give vent to a wonderful imitation of the lonely call of the coyote.

The Piccaninnies, on their part, trusted implicitly to his honour, and their whole action of the night stands out in marked contrast to his. They left nothing undone that was consistent with the reputation of their tribe. They knew

despicable [ˈdɛspɪkəb!] adj. 卑劣的
Consistent [kənˈsɪstənt] adj. 始終如一的

that the pirates were on the island from the moment one of them trod on a dry stick; and in an incredibly short space of time, the coyote cries began. Every foot of ground between the spot where Hook had landed his forces and the home under the trees was stealthily examined by braves wearing their moccasins with the heels in front. They found only one hillock with a stream at its base, so that Hook had no choice; here he must establish himself and wait for just before the dawn.

Everything being thus mapped out with almost diabolical cunning, the main body of the Indians folded their blankets around them, and in the phlegmatic manner that is to them the pearl of manhood squatted above the children's home, awaiting the cold moment when they should deal pale death.

Here dreaming, though wide-awake, of the exquisite tortures to which they were to put at the break of day, those confiding savages were found by the treacherous Hook. From the accounts afterwards supplied by such of the scouts as escaped the carnage, he does not seem even to

---

Establish [əˋstæblɪʃ] v. 設立；安置
Phlegmatic [flɛgˋmætɪk] adj. 冷淡的

have paused at the rising ground, though it is certain that in the grey light he must have seen it: no thought of waiting to be attacked appears from first to last to have visited his subtle mind; he would not even hold off till the night was nearly spent; he waged war immediately.

Around the brave Tiger Lily were a dozen of her stoutest warriors, and they suddenly saw the perfidious pirates bearing down upon them. Fell from their eyes then the film through which they had looked at victory. No more would they torture at the stake. For them the happy hunting-grounds now. They knew it; but as their fathers' sons they acquitted themselves. The tradition gallantly upheld, they seized their weapons, and the air was torn with the war-cry; but it was now too late.

The night's work was not yet over, for it was not the Indians Hook had come out to destroy; they were but the bees to be smoked, so that he should get at the honey. It was Pan he wanted, Pan and Wendy and their band, but chiefly Pan.

Peter was such a small boy that one tends to wonder at the man's hatred of him. True he had flung Hook's arm

Pause [pɔz] v. 停頓

to the crocodile, but even this and the increased insecurity of life to which it led, owing to the crocodile's pertinacity, hardly account for a vindictiveness so relentless and malignant. The truth is that there was a something about Peter which goaded the pirate captain to frenzy. It was not his courage, it was not his engaging appearance, it was not... There is no beating about the bush, for we know quite well what it was, and have got to tell. It was Peter's cockiness.

This had got on Hook's nerves; it made his iron claw twitch, and at night it disturbed him like an insect. While Peter lived, the tortured man felt that he was a lion in a cage into which a sparrow had come.

The question now was how to get down the trees, or how to get his dogs down? He ran his greedy eyes over them, searching for the thinnest ones. They wriggled uncomfortably, for they knew he would not scruple to ram them down with poles.

In the meantime, what of the boys? At the first clang of weapons, they turned as it were into stone figures, open-mouthed, all appealing with outstretched arms to Peter; and

Vindictiveness [vɪnˈdɪktɪvnɪs] n. 懷恨在心
Relentless [rɪˈlɛntlɪs] adj. 持續的

as their mouths close, and their arms fall to their sides.

Which side had won?

The pirates, listening avidly at the mouths of the trees, heard the question put by every boy, and alas, they also heard Peter's answer.

"If the Indians have won," he said, "they will beat the tom-tom; it is always their sign of victory."

Now Smee had found the tom-tom, and was at that moment sitting on it. "You will never hear the tom-tom again," he muttered, but inaudibly of course, for strict silence had been enjoined. To his amazement Hook signed to him to beat the tom-tom, and slowly there came to Smee an understanding of the dreadful wickedness of the order. Never, probably, had this simple man admired Hook so much.

Twice Smee beat upon the instrument, and then stopped to listen gleefully. "The tom-tom," the miscreants heard Peter cry; "an Indian victory!"

The doomed children answered with a cheer that was music to the black hearts above, and almost immediately

Avidly [ˈævɪdlɪ] adv. 聽不見似地
Wickedness [ˈwɪkɪdnɪs] n. 邪惡

they repeated their good-byes to Peter. This puzzled the pirates, but all their other feelings were swallowed by a base delight that the enemy were about to come up the trees. They smirked at each other and rubbed their hands. Rapidly and silently Hook gave his orders: one man to each tree, and the others to arrange themselves in a line two yards apart.

Repeated [rɪˋpitɪd] adj. 再三的；屢次的

CHAPTER 12

DO YOU BELIEVE IN FAIRIES?

The first to emerge from his tree was Curly. He rose out of it into the arms of Cecco, who flung him to Smee, who flung him to Starkey, who flung him to Bill Jukes, who flung him to Noodler, and so he was tossed from one to another till he fell at the feet of the black pirate. All the boys were plucked from their trees in this ruthless manner; and several of them were in the air at a time, like bales of goods flung from hand to hand.

A different treatment was accorded to Wendy, who came last. With ironical politeness Hook raised his hat to her, and, offering her his arm, escorted her to the spot where the others were being gagged. He did it with such an air, he was so frightfully distingue, that she was too fascinated to cry out. She was only a little girl.

Emerge [ɪˈmɝdʒ] v. 出現
Treatment [ˈtritmənt] n. 待遇
Escort [ˈɛskɔrt] v. 護衛；護送

Had she haughtily unhanded him, she would have been hurled through the air like the others, and then Hook would probably not have been present at the tying of the children; and had he not been at the tying he would not have discovered Slightly's secret, and without the secret he could not presently have made his foul attempt on Peter's life.

They were tied to prevent their flying away, doubled up with their knees close to their ears; and for this job the black pirate had cut a rope into nine equal pieces. All went well with the trussing until Slightly's turn came, when he was found to be like those irritating parcels that use up all the string in going round and leave no tags with which to tie a knot. While his dogs were merely sweating because every time they tried to pack the unhappy lad tight in one part he bulged out in another, Hook's master mind had gone far beneath Slightly's surface, probing not for effects but for causes; and his exultation showed that he had found them. Slightly, white to the gills, knew that Hook had surprised his secret, which was this, that no boy so blown out could use a tree wherein an average man need stick.

Sufficient of this Hook guessed to persuade him that Peter at last lay at his mercy, but no word of the dark design

Exultation [ˌɛgzʌlˈteʃən] n. 洋洋得意

that now formed in the subterranean cav-erns of his mind crossed his lips; he merely signed that the captives were to be conveyed to the ship, and that he would be alone.

The first thing he did on finding himself alone in the fast falling night was to tiptoe to Slightly's tree, and make sure that it provided him with a passage. Then for long he remained brooding; his hat of ill omen on the sward, so that a gentle breeze which had arisen might play refreshingly through his hair.

There was no way of knowing, save by going down. Hook let his cloak slip softly to the ground, and then biting his lips till a lewd blood stood on them, he stepped into the tree.

He arrived unmolested at the foot of the shaft, and stood still again, biting at his breath, which had almost left him. As his eyes became accustomed to the dim light various objects in the home under the trees took shape; but the only one on which his greedy gaze rested, long sought for and found at last, was the great bed. On the bed lay Peter fast asleep.

Unaware of the tragedy being enacted above, Peter

Unmolested [ˌʌnməˈlɛstɪd] **adj.** 不受干擾的

had continued, for a little time after the children left, to play gaily on his pipes: no doubt rather a forlorn attempt to prove to himself that he did not care. Then he decided not to take his medicine, so as to grieve Wendy. Then he lay down on the bed outside the coverlet, to vex her still more; for she had always tucked them inside it, because you never know that you may not grow chilly at the turn of the night. Then he nearly cried; but it struck him how indignant she would be if he laughed instead; so he laughed a haughty laugh and fell asleep in the middle of it.

Sometimes, though not often, he had dreams, and they were more painful than the dreams of other boys. For hours he could not be separated from these dreams, though he wailed piteously in them. At such times it had been Wendy's custom to take him out of bed and sit with him on her lap, soothing him in dear ways of her own invention. But on this occasion he had fallen at once into a dreamless sleep. One arm dropped over the edge of the bed, one leg was arched, and the unfinished part of his laugh was stranded on his mouth, which was open, showing the little pearls.

Vex [vɛks] v. 使生氣

Piteously [ˈpɪtɪəslɪ] adv. 可憐地

Thus defenceless Hook found him. He stood silent at the foot of the tree looking across the chamber at his enemy. Did no feeling of compassion stir his sombre breast? The man was not wholly evil.

What stayed him was Peter's impertinent appearance as he slept. The open mouth, the drooping arm, the arched knee: they were such a personification of cockiness as, taken together, will never again one may hope be presented to eyes so sensitive to their offensiveness. They steeled Hook's heart. If his rage had broken him into a hundred pieces every one of them would have disregarded the incident, and leapt at the sleeper.

Though a light from the one lamp shone dimly on the bed Hook stood in darkness himself, and at the first stealthy step forward he discovered an obstacle, the door of Slightly's tree. It did not entirely fill the aperture, and he had been looking over it. Feeling for the catch, he found to his fury that it was low down, beyond his reach.

But what was that? The red in his eye had caught sight of Peter's medicine standing on a ledge within easy reach. He fathomed what it was straightway, and immediately he knew that the sleeper was in his power.

 Cockiness [ˋkɑkɪnɪs] **n.** 趾高氣揚

Five drops of this he now added to Peter's cup. His hand shook, but it was in exultation rather than in shame. As he did it he avoided glancing at the sleeper, but not lest pity should unnerve him; merely to avoid spilling. Then one long gloating look he cast upon his victim, and turning, wormed his way with difficulty up the tree. As he emerged at the top he looked the very spirit of evil breaking from its hole.

Peter slept on. The light guttered and went out, leaving the tenement in darkness; but still he slept. It must have been not less than ten o'clock by the crocodile, when he suddenly sat up in his bed, wakened by he knew not what. It was a soft cautious tapping on the door of his tree.

Soft and cautious, but in that stillness it was sinister. Peter felt for his dagger till his hand gripped it. Then he spoke.

"Who is that?"

"Let me in, Peter."

It was Tink, and quickly he unbarred to her. She flew in excitedly, her face flushed and her dress stained with mud.

"What is it?"

Gloating [ˈglotɪŋ] adj. 幸災樂禍的
Tenement [ˈtɛnəmənt] n. 棲息之所

"Oh, you could never guess!" she cried, and offered him three guesses. "Out with it!" he shouted, and in one ungrammatical sentence, as long as the ribbons conjurers pull from their mouths, she told of the capture of Wendy and the boys.

"I'll rescue her!" he cried, leaping at his weapons. As he leapt he thought of something he could do to please her. He could take his medicine.

His hand closed on the fatal draught.

"No!" shrieked Tinker Bell, who had heard Hook muttering about his deed as he sped through the forest.

"Why not?"

"It is poisoned."

"Poisoned! Who could have poisoned it?"

"Hook."

"Don't be silly. How could Hook have got down here?"

Alas, Tinker Bell could not explain this, for even she did not know the dark secret of Slightly's tree. Nevertheless Hook's words had left no room for doubt. The cup was poisoned.

"Besides," said Peter, quite believing himself, "I never fell asleep."

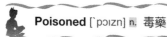
Poisoned [ˈpɔɪzn] n. 毒藥

He raised the cup. No time for words now; time for deeds, and with one of her lightning movements Tink got between his lips and the draught, and drained it to the dregs.

"Why, Tink, how dare you drink my medicine?"

But she did not answer. Already she was reeling in the air. "What is the matter with you?" cried Peter, suddenly afraid.

"It was poisoned, Peter," she told him softly; "and now I am going to be dead."

"Oh Tink, did you drink it to save me?"

"Yes."

"But why, Tink?"

Her wings would scarcely carry her now, but in reply she alighted on his shoulder and gave his nose a loving bite. She whispered in his ear "You silly ass," and then, tottering to her chamber, lay down on the bed.

His head almost filled the fourth wall of her little room as he knelt near her in distress. Every moment her light was growing fainter; and he knew that if it went out she would be no more. She liked his tears so much that she put out her beauti- ful finger and let them run over it.

Her voice was so low that at first he could not make out what she said. Then he made it out. She was saying that

she thought she could get well again if children believed in fairies.

Peter flung out his arms. There were no children there, and it was night time; but he addressed all who might be dreaming of the Neverland, and who were therefore nearer to him than you think: boys and girls in their nighties, and naked papooses in their baskets hung from trees.

"Do you believe?" he cried.

Tink sat up in bed almost briskly to listen to her fate.

She fancied she heard answers in the affirmative, and then again she wasn't sure.

"What do you think?" she asked Peter.

"If you believe," he shouted to them, "clap your hands; don't let Tink die." Many clapped.

Some didn't.

A few little beasts hissed.

The clapping stopped suddenly; as if countless mothers had rushed to their nurseries to see what on earth was happening; but already Tink was saved. First her voice grew strong, then she popped out of bed, then she was flashing through the room more merry and impudent than ever. She never thought of thanking those who believed, but she would have liked to get at the ones who had hissed.

"And now to rescue Wendy!"

The moon was riding in a cloudy heaven when Peter rose from his tree, begirt with weapons and wearing little else, to set out upon his perilous quest. It was not such a night as he would have chosen. He had hoped to fly, keeping not far from the ground so that nothing unwonted should escape his eyes; but in that fitful light to have flown low would have meant trailing his shadow through the trees, thus disturbing the birds and acquainting a watchful foe that he was astir.

The crocodile passed him, but not another living thing, not a sound, not a movement; and yet he knew well that sudden death might be at the next tree, or stalking him from behind.

He swore this terrible oath: "Hook or me this time."

CHAPTER 13

T HE PIRATE SHIP

One green light squinting over Kidd's Creek, which is near the mouth of the pirate river, marked where the brig, the Jolly Roger, lay, low in the water.

She was wrapped in the blanket of night, through which no sound from her could have reached the shore. There was little sound, and none agreeable save the whir of the ship's sewing machine at which Smee sat, ever industrious and obliging, the essence of the commonplace.

Hook trod the deck in thought. What an unfathomable man! It was his hour of triumph. Peter had been removed forever from his path, and all the other boys were on the brig, about to walk the plank.

Hook was not his true name. To reveal who he really was would even at this date set the country in a blaze; he had been at a famous public school; and its traditions still

Squinti [skwɪnt] **v.** 傾斜
Sewing [`soɪŋ] **n.** 縫級

clung to him like garments, with which indeed they are largely concerned. Thus it was offensive to him even now to board a ship in the same dress in which he grappled her, and he still adhered in his walk to the school's distinguished slouch. But above all he retained the passion for good form.

Good form! However much he may have degenerated, he still knew that this is all that really matters.

From far within him he heard a creaking as of rusty portals, and through them came a stern tap-tap-tap, like hammering in the night when one cannot sleep. "Have you been good form today?" was their eternal question.

Most disquieting reflection of all, was it not bad form to think about good form?

His vitals were tortured by this problem. It was a claw within him sharper than the iron one; and as it tore him, the perspiration dripped down his tallow countenance and streaked his doublet. Ofttimes he drew his sleeve across his face, but there was no damming that trickle.

There came to him a presentiment of his early dis-solution. It was as if Peter's terrible oath had boarded the

Distinguished [dɪ`stɪŋgwɪʃt] adj. 高貴的
Countenance [`kaʊntənəns] n. 面容

ship. Hook felt a gloomy desire to make his dying speech, lest presently there should be no time for it.

"No little children love me!"

Strange that he should think of this, which had never troubled him before; perhaps the sewing machine brought it to his mind. For long he muttered to himself, staring at Smee, who was hemming placidly, under the conviction that all children feared him.

Feared him! Feared Smee! There was not a child on board the brig that night who did not already love him. He had said horrid things to them and hit them with the palm of his hand, because he could not hit with his fist, but they had only clung to him the more. Michael had tried on his spectacles.

To tell poor Smee that they thought him lovable! Hook itched to do it, but it seemed too brutal. Instead, he revolved this mystery in his mind: why do they find Smee lovable? A terrible answer suddenly presented itself- "Good form?"

Had the bo'sun good form without knowing it, which is the best form of all?

Mutter [`mʌtə-] v. 低聲嘀咕

With a cry of rage he raised his iron hand over Smee's head; but he did not tear. What arrested him was this reflection:

"To claw a man because he is good form, what would that be?" "Bad form!"

The unhappy Hook was as impotent as he was damp, and he fell forward like a cut flower.

His dogs thinking him out of the way for a time, discipline instantly relaxed; and they broke into a bacchanalian dance, which brought him to his feet at once, all traces of human weakness gone, as if a bucket of water had passed over him.

"Quiet, you scugs," he cried, "or I'll cast anchor in you"; and at once the din was hushed. "Are all the children chained, so that they cannot fly away?"

"Ay, ay."

"Then hoist them up."

The wretched prisoners were dragged from the hold, all except Wendy, and ranged in line in front of him.

"Now then, bullies," he said briskly, "six of you walk

Impotent [ˈɪmpətənt] adj. 無能為力的

Hoist [hɔɪst] v. 吊起

the plank tonight, but I have room for two cabin boys. Which of you is it to be?"

"Don't irritate him unnecessarily," had been Wendy's instructions in the hold; so Tootles stepped forward politely. Tootles hated the idea of signing under such a man, but an instinct told him that it would be prudent to lay the responsibility on an absent person.

So Tootles explained prudently, "You see, sir, I don't think my mother would like me to be a pirate. Would your mother like you to be a pirate, Slightly?"

He winked at Slightly, who said mournfully, "I don't think so," as if he wished things had been otherwise.

"Stow this gab," roared Hook, and the spokesmen were dragged back. "You, boy," he said, addressing John, "you look as if you had a little pluck in you. Haven't you never wanted to be a pirate, my hearty?"

Now John had sometimes experienced this hankering at; and he was struck by Hook's picking him out.

"I once thought of calling myself Red-handed Jack," he said diffidently. "And a good name too. We'll call you that here, bully, if you join." "What do you think, Michael?"

Pluck [plʌk] *v.* 拔；扯

asked John.

"What would you call me if I join?" Michael demanded. "Blackbeard Joe"

Michael was naturally impressed. "What do you think, John?" He wanted John to decide, and John wanted him to decide.

"Shall we still be respectful subjects of the King?" John inquired.

Through Hook's teeth came the answer: "You would have to swear, 'Down with the King.'"

"Then I refuse!" he cried, banging the barrel in front of Hook.

"And I refuse," cried Michael. "Rule Britannia!" squeaked Curly.

The infuriated pirates buffeted them in the mouth; and Hook roared out, "That seals your doom. Bring up their mother. Get the plank ready."

They were only boys, and they went white as they saw Jukes and Cecco preparing the fatal plank. But they tried to look brave when Wendy was brought up.

To the boys there was at least some glamour in the

Glamour [ˈglæməˌ] **n.** 誘惑力

pirate calling; but all that she saw was that the ship had not been tidied for years. There was not a porthole on the grimy glass of which you might not have written with your finger "Dirty pig"; and she had already written it on several. But as the boys gathered round her she had no thought, of course, save for them.

"So, my beauty," said Hook, as if he spoke in syrup, "you are to see your children walk the plank."

"Are they to die?" asked Wendy, with a look of such frightful contempt that he nearly fainted.

"They are," he snarled. "Silence all," he called gloatingly, "for a mother's last words to her children."

At this moment Wendy was grand. "These are my last words, dear boys," she said firmly. "I feel that I have a message to you from your real mothers, and it is this: 'We hope our sons will die like English gentlemen.'"

Even the pirates were awed, and Tootles cried out hysterically, "I am going to do what my mother hopes. What are you to do, Nibs?"

"What my mother hopes. What are you to do, Twin?"

"What my mother hopes. John, what are-"

But Hook had found his voice again. "Tie her up!" he shouted.

It was Smee who tied her to the mast. "See here, honey," he whispered, "I'll save you if you promise to be my mother."

But not even for Smee would she make such a promise. "I would almost rather have no children at all," she said disdainfully.

It is sad to know that not a boy was looking at her as Smee tied her to the mast; the eyes of all were on the plank: that last little walk they were about to take. They were no longer able to hope that they would walk it manfully, for the capacity to think had gone from them; they could stare and shiver only.

Hook smiled on them with his teeth closed, and took a step toward Wendy. His intention was to turn her face so that she should see the boys walking the plank one by one. But he never reached her, he never heard the cry of anguish he hoped to wring from her. He heard something else instead.

It was the terrible tick-tick of the crocodile.

"Hide me!" he cried hoarsely.

They gathered round him, all eyes averted from the thing that was coming aboard. They had no thought of fighting it. It was Fate.

 Anguish [ˋæŋgwɪʃ] n. 極度的痛苦

Only when Hook was hidden from them did curiosity loosen the limbs of the boys so that they could rush to the ship's side to see the crocodile climbing it.

Then they got the strangest surprise of this Night of Nights; for it was no crocodile that was coming to their aid. It was Peter.

He signed to them not to give vent to any cry of admiration that might arouse suspicion. Then he went on ticking.

CHAPTER 14

"HOOK OR ME THIS TIME"

The last time we saw him he was stealing across the island with one finger to his lips and his dagger at the ready. he had seen the crocodile pass by without noticing anything peculiar about it, but by and by he remembered that it had not been ticking. At first he thought this eerie, but soon he concluded rightly that the clock had run down.

Without giving a thought to what might be the feelings of a fellow-creature thus abruptly deprived of its closest companion, Peter began to consider how he could turn the catastrophe to his own use; and he decided to tick, so that wild beasts should believe he was the crocodile and let him pass unmolested. He ticked superbly, but with one unforeseen result. The crocodile was among those who heard the sound, and it followed him.

Peter reached the shore without mishap, and went straight on, his legs encountering the water as if quite

Abruptly [əˋbrʌptlɪ] adv. 突然地

encounter [ɪnˋkaʊntɚ] v. 遭遇（敵人）；遇到（困難，危險等）

unaware that they had entered a new element. As he swam he had but one thought: "Hook or me this time." He had ticked so long that he now went on ticking without knowing that he was doing it.

On the contrary, he thought he had scaled her side as noiseless as a mouse; and he was amazed to see the pirates cowering from him, with Hook in their midst as abject as if he had heard the crocodile.

The crocodile! No sooner did Peter remember it than he heard the ticking. "How clever of me!" he thought at once, and signed to the boys not to burst into applause.

It was at this moment that Ed Teynte the quartermaster emerged from the forecastle and came along the deck. Peter struck true and deep. John clapped his hands on the ill-fated pirate's mouth to stifle the dying groan. He fell forward. Four boys caught him to prevent the thud. Peter gave the signal, and the carrion was cast overboard. There was a splash, and then silence.

None too soon, Peter, every inch of him on tip-toe, vanished into the cabin; for more than one pirate was screwing up his courage to look round. They could hear

 Abject [ˋæbdʒɛkt] adj. 糟透的；難堪的

each other's distressed breathing now, which showed them that the more terrible sound had passed.

"It's gone, captain," Smee said, wiping his spectacles. "All still again."

Slowly Hook let his head emerge from his ruff, and listened so intently that he could have caught the echo of the tick. There was not a sound, and he drew himself up firmly to his full height.

"Then here's to Johnny Plank!" he cried brazenly, hating the boys more than ever because they had seen him unbend.

To terrorise the prisoners the more, though with a certain loss of dignity, he danced along an imaginary plank, grimacing at them as he sang; and when he finished he cried, "Do you want a touch of the cat before you walk the plank?"

At that they fell on their knees. "No, no!" they cried so piteously that every pirate smiled.

"Fetch the cat, Jukes," said Hook, "it's in the cabin."

The cabin! Peter was in the cabin! The children gazed at each other.

"Ay, ay," said Jukes blithely, and he strode into the cabin. They followed him with their eyes.

It wailed through the ship, and died away. Then was heard a crowing sound which was well understood by the

boys, but to the pirates was almost much eerier than the screech.

"What was that?" cried Hook.

The Italian Cecco hesitated for a moment and then swung into the cabin. He tottered out, haggard.

"What's the matter with Bill Jukes, you dog?" hissed Hook, towering over him.

"The matter wi' him is he's dead, stabbed," replied Cecco in a hollow voice.

"Bill Jukes dead!" cried the startled pirates.

"Cecco," he said in his most steely voice, "go back and fetch me out that doo- dle-doo"

Cecco, bravest of the brave, cowered before his captain, crying, "No, no"; but Hook was purring to his claw.

"Did you say you would go, Cecco?" he said musingly.

Cecco went, first flinging up his arms despairingly. There was no more singing, all listened now; and again came a death-screech and again a crow.

Hook rallied his dogs with a gesture. "S' death and odds fish," he thundered, "who is to bring me that doodle-doo?"

"Wait till Cecco comes out," growled Starkey, and the

Hesitate [ˈhɛzəˌtet] v. 猶豫
Despairingly [dɪˈspɛrɪŋlɪ] adv. 絕望地

others took up the cry. "I think I heard you volunteer, Starkey," said Hook, purring again.

"No, by thunder!" Starkey cried.

"My hook thinks you did," said Hook, crossing to him. "I wonder if it would not be advisable, Starkey, to humour the hook?"

"I'll swing before I go in there," replied Starkey doggedly, and again he had the support of the crew.

"Is it mutiny?" asked Hook more pleasantly than ever. "Starkey's ringleader!" "Captain, mercy!" Starkey whimpered, all of a tremble now.

"Shake hands, Starkey," said Hook, proffering his claw.

Starkey looked round for help, but all deserted him. As he backed Hook advanced, and now the red spark was in his eye. With a despairing scream the pirate leapt upon Long Tom and precipitated himself into the sea.

"And now," Hook asked courteously, "did any other gentleman say mutiny?" Seizing a lantern and raising his claw with a menacing gesture, "I'll bring out that doodle-doo myself," he said, and sped into the cabin.

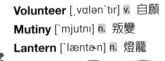

Volunteer [ˌvɑlən`tɪr] **v.** 自願
Mutiny [`mjutnɪ] **n.** 叛變
Lantern [`læntɚn] **n.** 燈籠

Hook came staggering out, without his lantern.

"Something blew out the light," he said a little unsteadily.

"What of Cecco?" demanded Noodler. "He's as dead as Jukes," said Hook shortly.

His reluctance to return to the cabin impressed them all unfavourably, and the mutinous sounds again broke forth. All pirates are superstitious, and Cookson cried, "They do say the surest sign a ship's accurst is when there's one on board more than can be accounted for."

"They say," said another, looking viciously at Hook, "that when he comes it's in the likeness of the wickedest man aboard"

"Had he a hook, captain?" asked Cookson insolently; and one after another took up the cry, "The ship's doomed!" At this the children could not resist raising a cheer. Hook had well-nigh forgotten his prisoners, but as he swung round on them now his face lit up again.

"Lads," he cried to his crew, "here's a notion. Open the cabin door and drive them in. Let them fight the doodle-doo for their lives. If they kill him, we're so much the

Viciously ['vɪʃəslɪ] adv. 猛烈地

Doomed [dumd] adj. 天數已盡的；在劫難逃的

better; if he kills them, we're none the worse."

For the last time his dogs admired Hook, and devotedly they did his bidding.

The boys, pretending to struggle, were pushed into the cabin and the door was closed on them.

"Now, listen!" cried Hook, and all listened. But not one dared to face the door. Yes, one, Wendy, who all this time had been bound to the mast. It was for neither a scream nor a crow that she was watching, it was for the reappearance of Peter.

She had not long to wait. In the cabin he had found the thing for which he had gone in search: the key that would free the children of their manacles, and now they all stole forth, armed with such weapons as they could find. First signing to them to hide, Peter cut Wendy's bonds, and then nothing could have been easier than for them all to fly off together; but one thing barred the way, an oath, "Hook or me this time." So when he had freed Wendy, he whispered to her to conceal herself with the others, and himself took her place by the mast, her cloak around him so that he should pass for her. Then he took a great breath and crowed.

Reappearance [ˌriəˈpɪrəns] n. 再現

To the pirates it was a voice crying that all the boys lay slain in the cabin; and they were panic-stricken. Hook tried to hearten them, but like the dogs he had made them they showed him their fangs.

"Lads," he said, ready to cajole or strike as need be, but never quailing for an instant, "I've thought it out. There's a Jonah aboard."

"Ay," they snarled, "a man wi' a hook"

"No, lads, no, it's the girl. Never was luck on a pirate ship wi' a woman on board. We'll right the ship when she's gone."

Some of them remembered that this had been a saying of Flint's. "It's worth trying," they said doubtfully.

"Fling the girl overboard," cried Hook; and they made a rush at the figure in the cloak.

"There's no one can save you now, missy," Mullins hissed jeeringly. "There's one," replied the figure.

"Who's that?"

"Peter Pan the avenger!" came the terrible answer; and as he spoke Peter flung off his cloak.

Hook cried, "Cleave him to the brisket!" but without conviction.

 Panic-stricken [ˈpænɪkˌstrɪkən] adj. 驚慌失措的

"Down, boys, and at them!" Peter's voice rang out; and in another moment the clash of arms was resounding through the ship. The pirates were stronger, but the boys were smarter and fought in airs. Some of the pirates jumped overboard, while others ran away and hid. Some of the miscreants leapt into the sea, others hid in dark recesses, where they were found by Slightly, who did not fight, but ran about with a lantern which he flashed in their faces, so that they were half blinded and fell an easy prey to the reeking swords of the other boys.

Finally only Hook was left. The boys surrounded him.

Again and again they closed upon him, and again and again he hewed a clear space. He had lifted up one boy with his hook, and was using him as a buckler, when another, who had just passed his sword through Mullins, sprang into the fray.

"Put up your swords, boys," cried the newcomer, "this man is mine"

Thus suddenly Hook found himself face to face with Peter. The others drew back and formed a ring round them.

For long the two enemies looked at one another, Hook shuddering slightly, and Peter with the strange smile upon his face.

"So, Pan," said Hook at last, "this is all your doing."

"Ay, James Hook," came the stern answer, "it is all my doing." "Proud and insolent youth," said Hook, "prepare to meet the doom." "Dark and sinister man," Peter answered, "Take that."

A dramatic sword fight followed, during which both man and boy fought bravely. Hook, scarcely his inferior in brilliancy, but not quite so nimble in wrist play, forced him back by the weight of his onset, hoping suddenly to end all with a favourite thrust, taught him long ago by Barbecue at Rio; but Peter doubled under it and, lunging fiercely, pierced him in the ribs. At sight of his own blood, whose peculiar colour, you remember, was offensive to him, the sword fell from Hook's hand, and he was at Peter's mercy.

"Now!" cried all the boys, but with a magnificent gesture Peter invited his opponent to pick up his sword. Hook did so instantly, but with a tragic feeling that Peter was showing good form.

He had been thinking it was some fiend fighting him, but darker suspicions assailed him now.

"Pan, who and what art thou?" he cried huskily.

Insolent [ˈɪnsələnt] adj. 無禮的
Sinister [ˈsɪnɪstɚ] adj. 陰險的

"I'm youth, I'm joy," Peter answered at a venture, "I'm a little bird that has broken out of the egg."

This, of course, was nonsense; but it was proof to the unhappy Hook that Peter did not know in the least who or what he was, which is the very pinnacle of good form.

"To't again," he cried despairingly.

He fought now like a human flail, and every sweep of that terrible sword would have severed in twain any man or boy who obstructed it; but Peter fluttered round him as if the very wind it made blew him out of the danger zone. And again and again he darted in and pricked.

Hook was fighting now without hope. That passionate breast no longer asked for life; but for one boon it craved: to see Peter bad form before it was cold forever.

Abandoning the fight he rushed into the powder magazine and fired it. "In two minutes," he cried, "the ship will be blown to pieces."

But Peter issued from the powder magazine with the shell in his hands, and calmly flung it overboard.

What sort of form was Hook himself showing? The other boys were flying around him now, flouting, scornful;

Pinnacle [ˋpɪnək!] n. 頂峰：極點

Obstruct [əbˋstrʌkt] v. 妨礙，阻擾

and as he staggered about the deck striking up at them impotently, his mind was no longer with them.

Seeing Peter slowly advancing upon him through the air with dagger poised, he sprang upon the bulwarks to cast himself into the sea. He did not know that the crocodile was waiting for him. Thus perished James Hook.

With the fight at last over, Wendy emerged from the cabin below. She praised them equally, and shuddered delightfully when Michael showed her the place where he had killed one; and then she took them into Hook's cabin and pointed to his watch which was hanging on a nail. It said "half-past one"!

The lateness of the hour was almost the biggest thing of all. She got them to bed in the pirates' bunks pretty quickly, you may be sure; all but Peter, who strutted up and down on deck, until at last he fell asleep by the side of Long Tom. He had one of his dreams that night, and cried in his sleep for a long time, and Wendy held him tight.

Praise [prez] n. 讚揚；稱讚

CHAPTER 15

THE RETURN HOME

The only change to be seen in the night-nursery is that between nine and six the kennel is no longer there. When the children flew away, Mr. Darling felt in his bones that all the blame was his for having chained Nana up, and that from first to last she had been wiser than he.

In the bitterness of his remorse he swore that he would never leave the kennel until his children came back.

Very touching was his deference to Nana. He would not let her come into the kennel, but on all other matters he followed her wishes implicitly.

Every morning the kennel was carried with Mr. Darling in it to a cab, which conveyed him to his office, and he returned home in the same way at six. Something of the strength of character of the man will be seen if we remember how sensitive he was to the opinion of

Remorse [rɪˈmɔrs] n. 痛悔

neighbours: this man whose every movement now attracted surprised attention.

It may have been quixotic, but it was magnificent. Soon the inward meaning of it leaked out, and the great heart of the public was touched.

Mrs. Darling was in the night-nursery awaiting George's return home: a very sad-eyed woman. Look at her in her chair, where she has fallen asleep. Her hand moves restlessly on her breast as if she had a pain there.

She has started up, calling their names; and there is no one in the room but Nana.

"Oh Nana, I dreamt my dear ones had come back."

Nana had filmy eyes, but all she could do was to put her paw gently on her mistress's lap, and they were sitting together thus when the kennel was brought back. As Mr. Darling puts his head out to kiss his wife, we see that his face is more worn than of yore, but has a softer expression.

For some time he sat with his head out of the kennel, talking with Mrs. Darling of this success, and pressing her hand reassuringly when she said she hoped his head would not be turned by it. Social success had not spoilt him; it had made him sweeter.

 Quixotic [kwɪkˋsɑtɪk] adj. 狂想的；異想天開的

"Won't you play me to sleep," he asked, "on the nursery piano?" and as she was crossing to the day-nursery he added thoughtlessly, "and shut that window. I feel a draught."

"Oh George, never ask me to do that. The window must always be left open for them, always, always."

Now it was his turn to beg her pardon; and she went into the day-nursery and played, and soon he was asleep; and while he slept, Peter and Tinker Bell flew into the room.

"Quick, Tink," he whispered, "close the window; bar it! That's right. Now you and I must get away by the door; and when Wendy comes she will think her mother has barred her out, and she will have to go back with me."

Instead of feeling that he was behaving badly he danced with glee; then he peeped into the day-nursery to see who was playing. He whispered to Tink, "It's Wendy's mother!"

He peeped in again to see why the music had stopped, and now he saw that Mrs. Darling had laid her head on the box, and that two tears were sitting on her eyes.

"She wants me to unbar the window," thought Peter, "but I won't, never!"

He peeped again, and the tears were still there, or

Draught [dræft] n. 通風氣流

another two had taken their place.

"She's awfully fond of Wendy," he said to himself. He was angry with her now for not seeing why she could not have Wendy.

I need her, too! he wanted to shout. **We can't both have her.**

He ceased to look at her, but even then she would not let go of him. He skipped about and made funny faces, but when he stopped it was just as if she were inside him, knocking.

"Oh, all right," he said at last, and gulped. Then he unbarred the window. "Come on, Tink," he cried, with a frightful sneer at the laws of nature: "we don't want any silly mothers", and he flew away.

Thus Wendy and John and Michael found the window open for them after all, which of course was more than they deserved. They alighted on the floor, quite unashamed of themselves, and the youngest one had already forgotten his home.

"I say," cried John, "the kennel!" and he dashed across to look into it. "Perhaps Nana is inside it," Wendy said.

But John whistled. "Hullo," he said, "there's a man

Deserved [dɪˈzɜ˞vd] **adj.** 應得的

inside it." "It's father!" exclaimed Wendy.

"Let me see father." Michael begged eagerly, and he took a good look. "He is not so big as the pirate I killed," he said with such frank disappointment that I am glad Mr. Darling was asleep; it would have been sad if those had been the first words he heard his little Michael say.

Wendy and John had been taken aback somewhat at finding their father in the kennel.

"Surely," said John, like one who had lost faith in his memory, "he used not to sleep in the kennel?"

"John," Wendy said falteringly, "perhaps we don't remember the old life as well as we thought we did."

A chill fell upon them; and serve them right.

"It is very careless of mother," said the young scoundrel John, "not to be here when we come back."

It was then that Mrs. Darling began playing again.

"It's mother!" cried Wendy, peeping. "So it is!" said John.

"Then are you not really our mother, Wendy?" asked Michael, who was surely sleepy.

"Oh dear!" exclaimed Wendy, with her first real twinge of remorse, "it was quite time we came back."

Twinge [twɪndʒ] n. 痛苦

"Let us creep in," John suggested, "and put our hands over her eyes."

But Wendy, who saw that they must break the joyous news more gently, had a better plan.

"Let us all slip into our beds, and be there when she comes in, just as if we had never been away."

And so when Mrs. Darling went back to the night-nursery to see if her husband was asleep, all the beds were occupied. The children waited for her cry of joy, but it did not come. She saw them, but she did not believe they were there.

She sat down in the chair by the fire, where in the old days she had nursed them.

"George, George!" she cried when she could speak; and Mr. Darling woke to share her bliss, and Nana came rushing in. There could not have been a lovelier sight; but there was none to see it except a little boy who was staring in at the window. He had ecstasies innumerable that other children can never know; but he was looking through the window at the one joy from which he must be forever barred.

Innumerable [ɪ`njumərəb!] adj. 無數的

CHAPTER 16

WHEN WENDY GREW UP

I hope you want to know what became of the other boys. They went up by the stair, because they thought this would make a better impression. They stood in a row in front of Mrs. Darling, with their hats off, and wishing they were not wearing their pirate clothes. They said nothing, but their eyes asked her to have them. They ought to have looked at Mr. Darling also, but they forgot about him.

Of course Mrs. Darling said at once that she would have them; but Mr. Darling was curiously depressed, and they saw that he considered six a rather large number.

The first twin was the proud one, and he asked, flushing, "Do you think we should be too much of a handful, sir? Because if so we can go away."

"Father!" Wendy cried, shocked.

"George!" Mrs. Darling exclaimed, pained to see her dear one showing himself in such an unfavourable light.

 Impression [ɪmˋprɛʃən] n. 印象

Then he burst into tears, and the truth came out. He
was as glad to have them as she was, he said, but he thought
they should have asked his consent as well as hers, instead
of treating him as a cypher in his own house.

"I don't think he is a cypher," Tootles cried instantly.
"Do you think he is a cypher, Curly?"

"No I don't. Do you think he is a cypher, Slightly?"
"Rather not. Twin, what do you think?"

It turned out that not one of them thought him a
cypher; and he was absurdly gratified, and said he would
find space for them all in the drawing-room if they fitted in.

"We'll fit in, sir," they assured him.

He went off dancing through the house, and they all
cried "Hoop la!" and danced after him, searching for the
drawing-room.

As for Peter, he saw Wendy once again before he
flew away. He did not exactly come to the window, but he
brushed against it in passing, so that she could open it if
she liked and call to him. That was what she did.

"Hullo, Wendy, good-bye," he said.

Burst into [bɜst ˋɪntu] phr. 突然
Cypher [ˋsaɪfə] n. 無價值的人

"Peter," she said falteringly, "that you would like to say anything to my parents about a very sweet subject?"

Mrs. Darling came to the window, for at present she was keeping a sharp eye on Wendy. She told Peter that she had adopted all the other boys, and would like to adopt him also.

"Would you send me to school?" he inquired craftily. "Yes."

"And then to an office?" "I suppose so."

"Soon I should be a man?"

"Very soon."

"I don't want to go to school and learn solemn things," he told her passionately. "I don't want to be a man. Oh Wendy's, mother, if I was to wake up and feel there was a beard!"

"Peter," said Wendy the comforter, "I should love you in a beard;" and Mrs. Darling stretched out her arms to him, but he repulsed her.

"Keep back, lady, no one is going to catch me and make me a man." "But where are you going to live?"

Adopted [əˈdɑptɪd] adj. 收養的
Beard [bɪrd] n. 鬍鬚

"With Tink in the house we built for Wendy. The fairies are to put it high up among the tree tops where they sleep at nights."

"How lovely," cried Wendy so longingly that Mrs. Darling tightened her grip. "I thought all the fairies were dead," Mrs. Darling said.

"There are always a lot of young ones," explained Wendy, who was now quite an authority, "because you see when a new baby laughs for the first time a new fairy is born, and as there are always new babies there are always new fairies."

They live in nests on the tops of trees; and the mauve ones are boys and the white ones are girls, and the blue ones are just little sillies who are not sure what they are."

"I shall have such fun," said Peter, looking at Wendy.

"It will be rather lonely in the evening," she said, "sitting by the fire."

"I shall have Tink."

"Tink can't go a twentieth part of the way round," she reminded him a little tartly.

"Well, then, come with me to the little house." "May I,

Authority [əˈθɔrətɪ] **n.** 權威人士；專家
Mauve [mov] **adj.** 淡紫色的

mummy?"

"Certainly not. I have got you home again, and I mean to keep you."

"Oh, all right," Peter said, as if he had asked her from politeness merely; but Mrs. Darling saw his mouth twitch, and she made this handsome offer: to let Wendy go to him for a week every year and do his spring cleaning.

"You won't forget me, Peter, will you, before spring-cleaning time comes?"

Of course Peter promised, and then he flew away. He took Mrs. Darling's kiss with him. The kiss that had been for no one else Peter took quite easily.

Of course all the boys went to school. A week before they had attended school they saw what goats they had been not to remain on the island; but it was too late now. It is sad to have to say that the power to fly gradually left them. In time they could not even fly after their hats. Want of practice, they called it; but what it really meant was that they no longer believed.

Michael believed longer than the other boys, though they jeered at him; so he was with Wendy when Peter came for her at the end of the first year. She flew away with Peter in the frock she had woven from leaves and berries in the Neverland, and her one fear was that he might notice how

short it had become, but he never noticed, he had so much to say about himself.

She had looked forward to thrilling talks with him about old times, but new adventures had crowded the old ones from his mind.

"Who is Captain Hook?" he asked with interest when she spoke of the arch enemy.

"Don't you remember," she asked, amazed,

"I forget them after I kill them," he replied carelessly.

When she expressed a doubtful hope that Tinker Bell would be glad to see her he said, "Who is Tinker Bell?"

"Oh Peter!" she said, shocked; but even when she explained he could not remember.

Wendy was pained to find that the past year was just like yesterday to Peter; it had seemed such a long year of waiting to her.

Next year he did not come for her. She waited in a new frock because the old one simply would not meet, but he never came.

"Perhaps he is ill," Michael said. "You know he is never

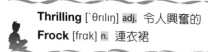

Thrilling [ˈθrɪlɪŋ] adj. 令人興奮的
Frock [frɑk] n. 連衣裙

ill."

Michael came close to her and whispered, with a shiver, "Perhaps there is no such person, Wendy!" and then Wendy would have cried if Michael had not been crying.

Peter came next spring cleaning; and the strange thing was that he never knew he had missed a year.

That was the last time the girl Wendy ever saw him. they met again Wendy was a married woman, and Peter was no more to her than a little dust in the box in which she had kept her toys. Wendy was grown up. You need not be sorry for her. She was one of the kind that likes to grow up. In the end she grew up of her own free will a day quicker than other girls.

All the boys were grown up and done for by this time.

Wendy was married in white with a pink sash. It is strange to think that Peter did not alight in the church and forbid the banns.

Years rolled on again, and Wendy had a daughter.

She was called Jane, and always had an odd inquiring look, as if from the mo- ment she arrived on the mainland she wanted to ask questions. When she was old enough to

Forbid [fə-'bɪd] v. 阻止；妨礙

ask them they were mostly about Peter Pan. She loved to hear of Peter, and Wendy told her all she could remember in the very nursery from which the famous flight had taken place. It was Jane's nursery now, for her father had bought it at the three percents from Wendy's father, who was no longer fond of stairs.

Mrs. Darling was now dead and forgotten.

There were only two beds in the nursery now, Jane's and her nurse's; and there was no kennel, for Nana also had passed away.

Once a week Jane's nurse had her evening off, and then it was Wendy's part to put Jane to bed. That was the time for stories. It was Jane's invention to raise the sheet over her mother's head and her own, thus making a tent, and in the awful darkness to whisper.

"What do we see now?"

"I don't think I see anything tonight," says Wendy, with a feeling that if Nana were here she would object to further conversation.

"Yes, you do," says Jane, "you see when you were a little

Invention [ɪnˈvɛnʃən] **n.** 發明，創造
Convention [kənˈvɛnʃən] **n.** 會議

girl."

"That is a long time ago, sweetheart," says Wendy. "Ah me, how time flies!" "Does it fly," asks the artful child, "the way you flew when you were a little girl?"

"The way I flew! Do you know, Jane, I sometimes wonder whether I ever did really fly."

"Yes, you did."

"The dear old days when I could fly!" "Why can't you fly now, mother?"

"Because I am grown up, dearest. When people grow up they forget the way." "Why do they forget the way?"

"Because they are no longer happy and innocent and heartless. It is only the happy and innocent and heartless who can fly."

"What is happy and innocent and heartless? I do wish I was happy and innocent and heartless."

Or perhaps Wendy admits she does see something. "I do believe," she says, "that it is this nursery!"

"I do believe it is!" says Jane. "Go on."

They are now embarked on the great adventure of the night when Peter flew in looking for his shadow.

"And then he flew us all away to the Neverland and the fairies and the pirates and the Indians and the mermaids'

lagoon, and the home under the ground, and the little house."

"Yes! which did you like best of all?"

"I think I liked the home under the ground best of all."

"Yes, so do I. What was the last thing Peter ever said to you?"

"The last thing he ever said to me was, 'Just always be waiting for me, and then some night you will hear me crowing.'"

"Yes!"

"But, alas, he forgot all about me." Wendy said it with a smile. She was as grown up as that.

"What did his crow sound like?" Jane asked one evening. "It was like this," Wendy said, trying to imitate Peter's crow.

"No, it wasn't," Jane said gravely, "it was like this"; and she did it ever so much better than her mother.

Wendy was a little startled. "My darling, how can you know?" "I often hear it when I am sleeping," Jane said.

"Ah yes, many girls hear it when they are sleeping, but I was the only one who heard it awake."

"Lucky you!" said Jane.

And then one night came the tragedy. It was the spring

of the year, and the story had been told for the night, and Jane was now asleep in her bed. Wendy was sitting on the floor, very close to the fire so as to see to darn, for there was no other light in the nursery; and while she sat darning she heard a crow. Then the window blew open as of old, and Peter dropped on the floor.

He was exactly the same as ever, and Wendy saw at once that he still had all his first teeth.

He was a little boy, and she was grown up. She huddled by the fire not daring to move, helpless and guilty, a big woman.

"Hullo, Wendy," he said, not noticing any difference, for he was thinking chiefly of himself; and in the dim light her white dress might have been the nightgown in which he had seen her first.

"Hullo, Peter," she replied faintly, squeezing herself as small as possible.

Peter looked. "Hullo, is it a new one?"

"Yes"

"Boy or girl?" "Girl."

Tragedy [ˈtrædʒədɪ] n. 悲劇性事件
Guilty [ˈɡɪltɪ] adj. 有罪的

Now surely he would understand; but not a bit of it.

"Peter," she said, faltering, "are you expecting me to fly away with you?" "Of course; that is why I have come" He added a little sternly, "Have you forgotten that this is spring-cleaning time?"

She knew it was useless to say that he had let many spring-cleaning times pass.

"I can't come," she said apologetically, "I have forgotten how to fly."

Then she turned up the light, and Peter saw. He gave a cry of pain; and when the tall beautiful creature stooped to lift him in her arms he drew back sharply.

"What is it?" he cried again.

She had to tell him.

"I am old, Peter. I am ever so much more than twenty. I grew up long ago." "You promised not to!"

"I couldn't help it. I am a married woman, Peter." "No, you're not"

"Yes, and the little girl in the bed is my baby."

"No, she's not."

But he supposed she was; and he took a step towards the sleeping child with his fist upraised. Of course he did

not strike her. He sat down on the floor and sobbed, and Wendy did not know how to comfort him, though she could have done it so easily once. She was only a woman now, and she ran out of the room to try to think.

Peter continued to cry, and soon his sobs woke Jane. She sat up in bed, and was interested at once.

When Wendy returned diffidently she found Peter sitting on the bedpost crowing gloriously, while Jane in her nighty was flying round the room in solemn ecstasy.

"Good-bye," said Peter to Wendy; and he rose in the air, and the shameless

Jane rose with him; it was already her easiest way of moving about.

Wendy rushed to the window. "No, no!" she cried.

"It is just for spring-cleaning time," Jane said; "he wants me always to do his spring cleaning."

"If only I could go with you!" Wendy sighed. "You see you can't fly," said Jane.

Of course in the end Wendy let them fly away together. Our last glimpse of her shows her at the window, watching

---

Upraised [ˌʌpˈrezd] adj. 舉起的

Gloriously [ˈglorɪəslɪ] adv. 壯觀地;壯麗地

them receding into the sky until they were as small as stars.

As you look at Wendy you may see her hair becoming white, and her figure little again, for all this happened long ago. Jane is now a common grown-up, with a daughter called Margaret; and every spring-cleaning time, except when he forgets, Peter comes for Margaret and takes her to the Neverland, where she tells him stories about himself, to which he listens eagerly. When Margaret grows up she will have a daughter, who is to be Peter's mother in turn; and so it will go on, so long as children are happy and innocent and heartless.

THE END

Glimpse [glɪmps] n. 瞥見